Johann Joachim Winckelmann, Henry Fuseli

Reflections on the Painting and Sculpture of the Greeks

with instructions for the connoisseur, and an essay on grace in works of art

Johann Joachim Winckelmann, Henry Fuseli

Reflections on the Painting and Sculpture of the Greeks
with instructions for the connoisseur, and an essay on grace in works of art

ISBN/EAN: 9783337734572

Printed in Europe, USA, Canada, Australia, Japan

Cover: Foto ©Andreas Hilbeck / pixelio.de

More available books at **www.hansebooks.com**

ON THE

PAINTING and SCULPTURE

OF

THE GREEKS:

WITH

INSTRUCTIONS for the CONNOISSEUR,

AND

An ESSAY on GRACE in Works of Art.

Tranſlated from

The *German* Original of the Abbé WINKELMANN,
Librarian of the VATICAN, F. R. S. &c. &c.

By HENRY FUSSELI, A. M.

LONDON:

Printed for the TRANSLATOR, and Sold by A. MILLAR,
in the Strand. 1765.

TO
The Lord SCARSDALE.

MY LORD,

WITH becoming gratitude for your Lordſhip's condeſcenſion in granting ſuch a noble Aſylum to a Stranger, I humbly preſume to ſhelter this Tranſlation under your Lordſhip's Patronage.

If I have been able to do juſtice to my Author, your Lordſhip's accurate Jugment, and fine Taſte, will naturally protect his Work: But I muſt rely wholly on your known

known Candour and Goodnefs for
the pardon of many imperfections
in the language.

I am, with the moſt profound
reſpect,

MY LORD,

YOUR LORDSHIP'S

Moſt obliged,

moſt obedient,

and moſt humble Servant,

LONDON,
10 April, 1765.

Henry Fuſſeli.

GRAIIS INGENIUM
&c.

ON THE

IMITATION

OF THE

PAINTING and SCULPTURE of
the GREEKS.

I. NATURE.

TO the Greek climate we owe the
production of TASTE, and from
thence it spread at length over all the politer
world. Every invention, communicated by
foreigners to that nation, was but the feed
of what it became afterwards, changing

B   both

both its nature and fize in a country, chofen, as *Plato* [a] fays, by Minerva, to be inhabited by the Greeks, as productive of every kind of genius.

But this TASTE was not only original among the Greeks, but feemed alfo quite peculiar to their country: it feldom went abroad without lofs; and was long ere it imparted its kind influences to more diftant climes. It was, doubtlefs, a ftranger to the northern zones, when Painting and Sculpture, thofe offsprings of Greece, were defpifed there to fuch a degree, that the moft valuable pieces of *Corregio* ferved only for blinds to the windows of the royal ftables at Stockholm.

There is but one way for the moderns to become great, and perhaps unequalled; I mean, by imitating the antients. And what we are told of *Homer*, that whoever underftands him well, admires him, we find no lefs true in matters concerning the antient, efpecially the Greek arts. But then we muft

[a] Plato in Timæc. Edit. Francof. p. 1044.

be

be as familiar with them as with a friend, to find Laocoon as inimitable as *Homer*. By fuch intimacy our judgment will be that of *Nicomachus : Take thefe eyes*, replied he to fome paltry critick, cenfuring the Helen of Zeuxis, *Take my eyes, and fhe will appear a goddefs.*

With fuch eyes *Michael Angelo, Raphael,* and *Pouffin,* confidered the performances of the antients.   They imbibed tafte at its fource ; and Raphael particularly in its native country.   We know, that he fent young artifts to Greece, to copy there, for his ufe, the remains of antiquity.

An antient Roman ftatue, compared to a Greek one, will generally appear like *Virgil*'s Diana amidft her Oreads, in comparifon of the Nauficaa of *Homer,* whom he imitated.

Laocoon was the ftandard of the Roman artifts, as well as ours ; and the rules of *Polycletus* became the rules of art.

I need not put the reader in mind of the negligences to be met with in the moft ce-

lebrated

lebrated antient performances : the Dolphin at the feet of the Medicean Venus, with the children, and the Parerga of the Diomedes by *Dioscorides,* being commonly known. The reverse of the best Egyptian and Syrian coins seldom equals the head, in point of workmanship.   Great artists are wisely negligent, and even their errors instruct.   Behold their works as *Lucian* bids you behold the Zeus of *Phidias*; *Zeus himself, not his footstool.*

It is not only *Nature* which the votaries of the Greeks find in their works, but still more, something superior to nature ; ideal beauties, brain-born images, as *Proclus* says [b].

The most beautiful body of ours would perhaps be as much inferior to the most beautiful Greek one, as Iphicles was to his brother Hercules.   The forms of the Greeks, prepared to beauty, by the influence of the mildest and purest sky, became perfectly elegant by their early exercises.   Take a

[b] In Timæum Platonis.

a Spar-

a Spartan youth, fprung from heroes, undiftorted by fwaddling-cloths; whofe bed,
from his feventh year, was the earth, familiar with wreftling and fwimming from his
infancy; and compare him with one of our
young Sybarits, and then decide which of
the two would be deemed worthy, by an
artift, to ferve for the model of a Thefeus,
an Achilles, or even a Bacchus. The latter would produce a Thefeus fed on rofes,
the former a Thefeus fed on flefh, to borrow
the expreffion of *Euphranor*.

The grand games were always a very
ftrong incentive for every Greek youth to
exercife himfelf. Whoever afpired to the
honours of thefe was obliged, by the laws, to
fubmit to a trial of ten months at Elis, the
general rendezvous; and there the firft rewards were commonly won by youths, as
Pindar tells us. ᶜ *To be like the God-like Di-
agoras,* was the fondeft wifh of every youth.

ᶜ Vide Pindar. Olymp. Od. VII. Arg. & Schol.

Behold the fwift Indian outftripping in purfuit the hart: how brifkly his juices circulate! how flexible, how elaftic his nerves and mufcles! how eafy his whole frame! Thus *Homer* draws his heroes, and his Achilles he eminently marks for " being fwift of foot."

By thefe exercifes the bodies of the Greeks ,got the great and manly Contour obferved in their ftatues, without any bloated corpulency. The young Spartans were bound to appear every tenth day naked before the Ephori, who, when they perceived any inclinable to fatnefs, ordered them a fcantier diet; nay, it was one of *Pythagoras's* precepts, to beware of growing too corpulent; and, perhaps for the fame reafon, youths afpiring to wreftling-games were, in the remoter ages of Greece, during their trial, confined to a milk diet.

They were particularly cautious in avoiding every deforming cuftom; and *Alcibiades,* when a boy, refufing to learn to play on

the

the flute, for fear of its difcompofing his features, was followed by all the youth of Athens.

In their drefs they were profeffed followers of nature. No modern ftiffening habit, no fqueezing ftays hindered Nature from forming eafy beauty ; the fair knew no anxiety about their attire, and from their loofe and fhort habits the Spartan girls got the epithet of Phænomirides.

We know what pains they took to have handfome children, but want to be acquainted with their methods: for certainly *Quillet*, in his Callipædy, falls fhort of their numerous expedients. They even attempted changing blue eyes to black ones, and games of beauty were exhibited at Elis, the rewards confifting of arms confecrated to the temple of Minerva. How could they mifs of competent and learned judges, when, as *Aristotle* tells us, the Grecian youths were taught drawing exprefsly for that purpofe? From their fine complexion, which, though ming-

B 4   led

led with a vaft deal of foreign blood, is ftill preferved in moft of the Greek iflands, and from the ftill enticing beauty of the fair fex, efpecially at Chios; we may eafily form an idea of the beauty of the former inhabitants, who boafted of being Aborigines, nay, more antient than the moon.

And are not there feveral modern nations, among whom beauty is too common to give any title to pre-eminence? Such are unanimoufly accounted the Georgians and the Kabardinfki in the Crim.

Thofe difeafes which are deftructive of beauty, were moreover unknown to the Greeks. There is not the leaft hint of the fmall-pox, in the writings of their phyficians; and *Homer*, whofe portraits are always fo truly drawn, mentions not one pitted face. Venereal plagues, and their daughter the Englifh malady, had not yet names.

And muft we not then, confidering every advantage which nature beftows, or art teaches, for forming, preferving, and improving beauty, enjoyed and applied by the Grecians; muſt we not then confeſs, there is the ſtrongeſt probability that the beauty of their perſons excelled all we can have an idea of?

Art claims liberty: in vain would nature produce her nobleſt offsprings, in a country where rigid laws would choak her progreſſive growth, as in Egypt, that pretended parent of ſciences and arts: but in Greece, where, from their earlieſt youth, the happy inhabitants were devoted to mirth and pleaſure, where narrow-ſpirited formality never reſtrained the liberty of manners, the artiſt enjoyed nature without a veil.

The Gymnaſies, where, ſheltered by public modeſty, the youths exerciſed themſelves naked, were the ſchools of art. Theſe the philoſopher frequented, as well as the artiſt. *Socrates* for the inſtruction of a Charmides, Autolycus, Lyſis; *Phidias* for the improvement of his art by their beauty. Here he ſtudied the elaſticity of the muſcles, the ever

vary-

varying motions of the frame, the outlines of fair forms, or the Contour left by the young wreſtler on the ſand. Here beautiful nakedneſs appeared with ſuch a livelineſs of expreſſion, ſuch truth and variety of ſituations, ſuch a noble air of the body, as it would be ridiculous to look for in any hired model of our academies.

Truth ſprings from the feelings of the heart. What ſhadow of it therefore can the modern artiſt hope for, by relying upon a vile model, whoſe ſoul is either too baſe to feel, or too ſtupid to expreſs the paſſions, the ſentiment his object claims? unhappy he! if experience and fancy fail him.

The beginning of many of *Plato*'s dialogues, ſuppoſed to have been held in the Gymnaſies, cannot raiſe our admiration of the generous ſouls of the Athenian youth, without giving us, at the ſame time, a ſtrong preſumption of a ſuitable nobleneſs in their outward carriage and bodily exerciſes.

The

The faireſt youths danced undreſſed on the theatre ; and *Sophocles*, the great *Sophocles*, when young, was the firſt who dared to entertain his fellow-citizens in this manner. *Phryne* went to bathe at the Eleuſinian games, expoſed to the eyes of all Greece, and riſing from the water became the model of Venus Anadyomene. During certain ſolemnities the young Spartan maidens danced naked before the young men : ſtrange this may ſeem, but will appear more probable, when we conſider that the chriſtians of the primitive church, both men and women, were dipped together in the ſame font.

Then every ſolemnity, every feſtival, afforded the artiſt opportunity to familiarize himſelf with all the beauties of Nature.

In the moſt happy times of their freedom, the humanity of the Greeks abhorred bloody games, which even in the Ionick Aſia had ceaſed long before, if, as ſome gueſs, they had once been uſual there. *Antiochus Epiphanes*, by ordering ſhews of Ro-

man

man gladiators, firſt preſented them with
ſuch unhappy victims; and cuſtom and
time, weakening the pangs of ſympathizing
humanity, changed even theſe games into
ſchools of art. There *Cteſias* ſtudied his
dying gladiator, in whom you might deſcry
" how much life was ſtill left in him ᵈ."

Theſe frequent occaſions of obſerving Nature, taught the Greeks to go on ſtill farther.
They began to form certain general ideas of
beauty, with regard to the proportions of
the inferiour parts, as well as of the whole
frame : theſe they raiſed above the reach of
mortality, according to the ſuperiour model
ˈof ſome ideal nature.

Thus *Raphael* formed his Galatea, as we
learn by his letter to Count Baltazar Caſtig-
lione ᵉ, where he ſays, " Beauty being ſo

ᵈ Some are of opinion, that the celebrated Ludo-
viſian gladiator, now in the great ſallon of the ca-
pitol, is this ſame whom Pliny mentions.

ᵉ Vide Bellori Deſcriz delle Imagini dipinte da
Raffaelle d'Vrbino, &c. Roma. 1695 fol.

ſeldom

feldom found among the fair, I avail myfelf
of a certain ideal image."

According to thofe ideas, exalted above
the pitch of material models, the Greeks
formed their gods and heroes: the profile of
the brow and nofe of gods and goddeffes is
almoft a ftreight line. The fame they gave
on their coins to queens, &c. but without
indulging their fancy too much. Perhaps
this profile was as peculiar to the antient
Greeks, as flat nofes and little eyes to the
Calmucks and Chinefe; a fuppofition which
receives fome ftrength from the large eyes
of all the heads on Greek coins and gems.

From the fame ideas the Romans formed their Empreffes on their coins. Livia
and Agrippina have the profile of Artemifia
and Cleopatra.

We obferve, neverthelefs, that the Greek
artifts in general, fubmitted to the law pre-
fcribed by the Thebans: " To do, under
a penalty, their beft in imitating Nature."
For, where they could not poffibly apply
their

their eafy profile, without endangering the refemblance, they followed Nature, as we fee inftanced in the beauteous head of Julia, the daughter of Titus, done by *Euodus*[c].

But to form a " juft refemblance, and, at the fame time, a handfomer one," being always the chief rule they obferved, and which *Polygnotus* conftantly went by; they muft, of neceffity, be fuppofed to have had in view a more beauteous and more perfect Nature.   And when we are told, that fome artifts imitated *Praxiteles*, who took his con-cubine *Cratina* for the model of his Cnidian Venus; or that others formed the graces from *Lais*; it is to be underftood that they did fo, without neglecting thefe great laws of the art.   Senfual beauty furnifhed the painter with all that nature could give ; ideal beauty with the awful and fublime ; from that he took the *Humane*, from this the *Divine*.

[c] Vide Stofch Pierres grav. pl. XXXIII.

Let any one, fagacious enough to pierce into the depths of art, compare the whole fyftem of the Greek figures with that of the moderns, by which, as they fay, nature alone is imitated; good heaven! what a number of neglected beauties will he not difcover!

For inftance, in moft of the modern figures, if the fkin happens to be any where preffed, you fee there feveral little fmart wrinkles: when, on the contrary, the fame parts, preffed in the fame manner on Greek ftatues, by their foft undulations, form at laft but one noble preffure. Thefe mafter-pieces never fhew us the fkin forcibly ftretched, but foftly embracing the firm flefh, which fills it up without any tumid expanfion, and harmonioufly follows its direction. There the fkin never, as on modern bodies, appears in plaits diftinct from the flefh.

Modern works are likewife diftinguifhed from the antient by parts; a crowd of fmall touches and dimples too fenfibly drawn. In antient works you find thefe diftributed with

fparing

sparing sagacity, and, as relative to a completer and more perfect Nature, offered but as hints, nay, often perceived only by the learned.

The probability still increases, that the bodies of the Greeks, as well as the works of their artists, were framed with more unity of system, a nobler harmony of parts, and a completeness of the whole, above our lean tensions and hollow wrinkles.

Probability, 'tis true, is all we can pretend to: but it deserves the attention of our artists and connoisseurs the rather, as the veneration professed for the antient monuments is commonly imputed to prejudice, and not to their excellence; as if the numerous ages, during which they have mouldered, were the only motive for bestowing on them exalted praises, and setting them up for the standards of imitation.

Such as would fain deny to the Greeks the advantages both of a more perfect Nature and of ideal Beauties, boast of the fa-

mous

mous *Bernini*, as their great champion. He was of opinion, besides, that Nature was possessed of every requisite beauty: the only skill being to discover that. He boasted of having got rid of a prejudice concerning the Medicean Venus, whose charms he at first thought peculiar ones; but, after many careful researches, discovered them now and then in Nature [s].

He was taught then, by the Venus, to discover beauties in common Nature, which he had formerly thought peculiar to that statue, and but for it, never would have searched for them. Follows it not from thence, that the beauties of the Greek statues being discovered with less difficulty than those of Nature, are of course more affecting; not so diffused, but more harmoniously united? and if this be true, the pointing out of Nature as chiefly imitable, is leading us into a more tedious and bewildered road to the

[s] Baldinucci Vita del Cav. Barnini.

C   know-

knowledge of perfect beauty, than setting up
the ancients for that purpose: consequently
Bernini, by adhering too strictly to Nature,
acted against his own principles, as well as
obstructed the progress of his disciples.

The imitation of beauty is either reduced
to a single object, and is *individual*, or, ga-
thering observations from single ones, *com-
poses of these one whole*. The former we call
copying, drawing a portrait; 'tis the straight
way to Dutch forms and figures; whereas
the other leads to general beauty, and its
ideal images, and is the way the Greeks took.
But there is still this difference between them
and us: they enjoying daily occasions of
seeing beauty, (suppose even not superior
to ours,) acquired those ideal riches with
less toil than we, confined as we are to a
few and often fruitless opportunities, ever
can hope for. It would be no easy matter,
I fancy, for our nature, to produce a frame
equal in beauty to that of Antinous; and

surely

furely no idea can foar above the more than human proportions of a deity, in the Apollo of the Vatican, which is a compound of the united force of Nature, Genius, and Art.

Their imitation difcovering in the one every beauty diffufed through Nature, fhewing in the other the pitch to which the moft perfect Nature can elevate herfelf, when foaring above the fenfes, will quicken the genius of the artift, and fhorten his difciplefhip: he will learn to think and draw with confidence, feeing here the fixed limits of human and divine beauty.

Building on this ground, his hand and fenfes directed by the Greek rule of beauty, the modern artift goes on the fureft way to the imitation of Nature. The ideas of unity and perfection, which he acquired in meditating on antiquity, will help him to combine, and to ennoble the more fcattered and weaker beauties of our Nature. Thus he will improve every beauty he difcovers in

it,

it, and by comparing the beauties of nature with the ideal, form rules for himfelf.

Then, and not fooner, he, particularly the painter, may be allowed to commit himfelf to Nature, efpecially in cafes where his art is beyond the inftruction of the old marbles, to wit, in drapery; then, like *Pouſſin*; he may proceed with more liberty; for " a " timid follower will never get the ftart of " his leaders, and he who is at a lofs to " produce fomething of his own, will be " a bad manager of the productions of an- " other;" as *Michael Angelo* fays, Minds favoured by Nature,

Quibus Arte benigna,
Et meliore luto, finxit præcordia Titan,

have here a plain way to become originals.

Thus the account *de Piles* gives, ought to be underftood, that *Raphael*, a fhort time before he was carried off by death, intended to forfake the marbles, in order to addict himfelf wholly to Nature.   True antient

tafte

tafte would moft certainly have guided him through every maze of common Nature; and whatever obfervations, whatever new ideas he might have reaped from that, they would all, by a kind of chymical tranfmutation, have been changed to his own effence and foul.

He, perhaps, might have indulged more variety; enlarged his draperies; improved his colours, his light and fhadow: but none of thefe improvements would have raifed his pictures to that high efteem they deferve, for that noble Contour, and that fublimity of thoughts, which he acquired from the ancients.

Nothing would more decifively prove the advantages to be got by imitating the ancients, preferably to Nature, than an effay made with two youths of equal talents, by devoting the one to antiquity, the other to Nature: this would draw Nature as he finds her; if Italian, perhaps he might paint like *Caravaggio*; if Flemifh, and lucky,

C 3   like

like *Jac. Jordans*; if French, like *Stella*: the other would draw her as fhe directs, and paint like *Raphael*.

II. Contour.

BUT even fuppofing that the imitation of Nâture could fupply all the artift wants, fhe never could beftow the precifion of Contour, that characteriftic diftinction of the ancients.

The nobleft Contour unites or circum-fcribes every part of the moft perfect Nature, and the ideal beauties in the figures of the Greeks; or rather, contains them both. *Euphranor*, famous after the epoch of *Zeuxis*, is faid to have firft ennobled it.

Many of the moderns have attempted to imitate this Contour, but very few with fuc-cefs. The great *Rubens* is far from having attained either its precifion or elegance, efpe-cially in the performances which he finifhed

before

before he went to Italy, and ſtudied the antiques.

The line by which Nature divides com-
pleteneſs from ſuperfluity is but a ſmall one,
and, inſenſible as it often is, has been croſſed
even by the beſt moderns; while theſe, in
ſhunning a meagre Contour, became corpulent, thoſe, in ſhunning that, grew lean.

Among them all, only *Michael Angelo,*
perhaps, may be ſaid to have attained the
antique; but only in ſtrong muſcular figures,
heroic frames; not in thoſe of tender youth;
nor in female bodies, which, under his bold
hand, grew Amazons.

The Greek artiſt, on the contrary, ad-
juſted his Contour, in every figure, to the
breadth of a ſingle hair, even in the niceſt
and moſt tireſome performances, as gems.
Conſider the Diomedes and Perſeus of *Dioſcorides*[h], Hercules and Iole by *Teucer*[i], and
admire the inimitable Greeks.

[h] Vide Stoſch Pierres Grav. pl. XXIX. XXX.
[i] Vide Muſ. Flor. T. II. t. V.

C 4   *Parrha-*

Parrhafius, they fay, was mafter of the correcteft Contour.

This Contour reigns in Greek figures, even when covered with drapery, as the chief aim of the artift; the beautiful frame pierces the marble like a tranfparent *Coan* cloth.

The high-ftiled Agrippina, and the three veftals in the royal cabinet at Drefden, deferve to be mentioned as eminent proofs of this. This Agrippina feems not the mother of Nero, but an elder one, the fpoufe of Germanicus. She much refembles another pretended Agrippina, in the parlour of the library of St. Marc, at Venice [k]. Ours is a fitting figure, above the fize of Nature, her head inclined on her right hand; her fine face fpeaks a foul " pining in thought," abforbed in penfive forrow, and fenfelefs to every outward impreffion. The artift, I fuppofe, intended to draw his heroine in the

[k] Vide Zanetti Statue nell' Antifala della libraria di S. Marco. Venez. 1740. fol.

mourn-

mournful moment fhe received the news of her banifhment to Pandataria.

The three veftals deferve our efteem from a double title: as being the firft important difcoveries of Herculaneum, and models of the fublimeft drapery. All three, but particularly one above the natural fize, would, with regard to that, be worthy companions of the Farnefian *Flora*, and all the other boafts of antiquity. The two others feem, by their refemblance to each other, productions of the fame hand, only diftinguifhed by their heads, which are not of equal goodnefs. On the beft the curled hairs, running in furrows from the forehead, are tied on the neck: on the other the hair being fmooth on the fcalp, and curled on the front, is gathered behind, and tied with a ribband: this head feems of a modern hand, but a good one.

There is no veil on thefe heads; but that makes not againft their being veftals: for the prieftefles of Vefta (I fpeak on proof)
were

were not always veiled; or rather, as the
drapery feems to betray, the veil, which
was of one piece with the garments, being
thrown backwards, mingles with the cloaths
on the neck.

'Tis to thefe three inimitable pieces that
the world owes the firft hints of the enfuing
difcovery of the fubterranean treafures of
Herculaneum.

Their difcovery happened when the
fame ruins that overwhelmed the town had
nearly extinguifhed the unhappy remembrance of it: when the tremendous fate that
fpoke its doom was only known by the account which Pliny gives of his uncle's
death.

Thefe great mafter-pieces of the Greek
art were tranfplanted, and worfhipped in Germany, long before Naples could boaft of one
fingle Herculanean monument.

They were difcovered in the year 1706 at
Portici near Naples, in a ruinous vault, on
occafion of digging the foundations of a

2   villa,

villa, for the Prince d'Elbeuf, and immediately, with other new difcovered marble
and metal ftatues, came into the poffeffion
of Prince Eugene, and were tranfported to
Vienna.

Eugene, who well knew their value, provided a Sala Terrena to be built exprefsly for
them, and a few others : and fo highly were
they efteemed, that even on the firft rumour
of their fale, the academy and the artifts
were in an uproar, and every body, when
they were tranfported to Drefden, followed
them with heavy eyes.

The famous *Matielli*, to whom

> *His rule Polyclet, his chiffel Phidias gave,*
>
> Algarotti.

copied them in clay before their removal,
and following them fome years after, filled
Drefden with everlafting monuments of his
art : but even there he ftudied the drapery
of his priefteffes, (drapery his chief fkill !)
till he laid down his chiffel, and thus gave
the

the moſt ſtriking proof of their excellence.

III. DRAPERY.

BY Drapery is to be underſtood all that the
art teaches of covering the nudities, and
folding the garments; and this is the third
prerogative of the ancients.

The Drapery of the veſtals above, is grand
and elegant. The ſmaller foldings ſpring gradually from the larger ones, and in them are
loſt again, with a noble freedom, and gentle harmony of the whole, without hiding
the correct Contour.   How few of the moderns would ſtand the teſt here!

Juſtice, however, ſhall not be refuſed to
ſome great modern artiſts, who, without im-
pairing nature or truth, have left, in certain
caſes, the road which the ancients generally
purſued. The Greek Drapery, in order
to help the Contour, was, for the moſt part,
taken from thin and wet garments, which of

3

courſe

courſe claſped the body, and diſcovered the ſhape. The robe of the Greek ladies was extremely thin; thence its epithet of Peplon.

Nevertheleſs the reliefs, the pictures, and particularly the buſts of the ancients, are inſtances that they did not always keep to this undulating Drapery [1].

In modern times the artiſts were forced to heap garments, and ſometimes heavy ones, on each other, which of courſe could not fall into the flowing folds of the ancients. Hence the large-folded Drapery, by which the painter and ſculptor may diſplay as much ſkill as by the ancient manner. *Carlo Marat* and *Francis Solimena* may be called the chief maſters of it: but the garments of the new Venetian ſchool, by paſſing the bounds of nature and propriety, became ſtiff as braſs.

[1] Among the buſts remarkable for that coarſer Drapery, we may reckon the beauteous Caracalla in the royal cabinet at Dreſden.

IV. Ex-

IV. EXPRESSION.

THE laſt and moſt eminent charaćteriſtic of the Greek works is a noble ſimplicity and ſedate grandeur in Geſture and Expreſſion.   As the bottom of the ſea lies peaceful beneath a foaming ſurface, a great ſoul lies ſedate beneath the ſtrife of paſſions in Greek figures.

'Tis in the face of Laocoon this ſoul ſhines with full luſtre, not confined however to the face, amidſt the moſt violent ſufferings.   Pangs piercing every muſcle, every labouring nerve; pangs which we almoſt feel ourſelves, while we conſider—not the face, nor the moſt expreſſive parts— only the belly contraćted by excruciating pains: theſe however, I ſay, exert not themſelves with violence, either in the face or geſture.   He pierces not heaven, like the Laocoon of *Virgil*; his mouth is rather opened to diſcharge an anxious overloaded

groan,

groan, as *Sadolet* fays; the ftruggling body and the fupporting mind exert themfelves with equal ftrength, nay balance all the frame.

Laocoon fuffers, but fuffers like the Philoctetes of *Sophocles*: we weeping feel his pains, but wifh for the hero's ftrength to fupport his mifery.

The Expreffion of fo great a foul is beyond the force of mere nature. It was in his own mind the artift was to fearch for the ftrength of fpirit with which he marked his marble. Greece enjoyed artifts and philofophers in the fame perfons; and the wifdom of more than one Metrodorus directed art, and infpired its figures with more than common fouls.

Had Laocoon been covered with a garb becoming an antient facrificer, his fufferings would have loft one half of their Expreffion. *Bernini* pretended to perceive the firft effects of the operating venom in the numbnefs of one of the thighs.

Every

Every action or gesture in Greek figures, not stamped with this character of sage dignity, but too violent, too passionate, was called " Parenthyrsos."

For, the more tranquillity reigns in a body, the fitter it is to draw the true character of the soul; which, in every exceffive gesture, feems to ruſh from her proper centre, and being hurried away by extremes becomes unnatural. Wound up to the higheſt pitch of paffion, ſhe may force herſelf upon the duller eye; but the true ſphere of her action is ſimplicity and calmnefs. In Laocoon ſufferings alone had been Parenthyrfos; the artiſt therefore, in order to reconcile the fignificative and ennobling qualities of his foul, put him into a poſture, allowing for the fufferings that were neceſſary, the next to a ſtate of tranquillity: a tranquillity however that is characteriſtical: the foul will be herſelf—this individual—not the foul of mankind; fedate, but active ; calm, but not indifferent or drowſy.

What

What a contraſt! how diametrically op-poſite to this is the taſte of our modern ar-tiſts, eſpecially the young ones! on nothing do they beſtow their approbation, but con-torſions and ſtrange poſtures, inſpired with boldneſs; this they pretend is done with ſpirit, with *Franchezza.* Contraſt is the darling of their ideas; in it they fancy every perfection. They fill their performances with comet-like excentric ſouls, deſpiſing every thing but an Ajax or a Capaneus.

Arts have their infancy as well as men; they begin, as well as the artiſt, with froth and bombaſt: in ſuch buſkins the muſe of Æſchilus ſtalks, and part of the diction in his Agamemnon is more loaded with hyper-boles than all Heraclitus's nonſenſe. Per-haps the primitive Greek painters drew in the ſame manner that their firſt good trage-dian thought in.

In all human actions flutter and raſh-neſs precede, ſedateneſs and ſolidity follow: but time only can diſcover, and the judi-

D   cious

cious will admire thefe only : they are the characteriftics of great mafters; violent paffions run away with their difciples.

The fages in the art know the difficulties hid under that air of eafinefs :

>   *ut fibi quivis*
> *Speret idem, fudet multum, fruftraque laboret*
> *Aufus idem.*   Hor.

La Fage, though an eminent defigner, was not able to attain the purity of ancient tafte. Every thing is animated in his works; they demand, and at the fame time diffipate, your attention, like a company ftriving to talk all at once.

This noble fimplicity and fedate grandeur is alfo the true characteriftical mark of the beft and matureft Greek writings, of the epoch and fchool of *Socrates*. Poffeffed of thefe qualities *Raphael* became eminently great, and he owed them to the ancients.

That great foul of his, lodged in a beauteous body, was requifite for the firft
difcovery

difcovery of the true character of the ancients: he firft felt all their beauties, and (what he was peculiarly happy in!) at an age when vulgar, unfeeling, and half-moulded fouls overlook every higher beauty.

Ye that approach his works, teach your eyes to be fenfible of thofe beauties, refine your tafte by the true antique, and then that folemn tranquillity of the chief figures in his *Attila*, deemed infipid by the vulgar, will appear to you equally fignificant and fublime. The Roman bifhop, in order to divert the Hun from his defign of affailing Rome, appears not with the air of a Rhetor, but as a venerable man, whofe very prefence foftens uproar into peace ; like him drawn by Virgil :

Tum pietate gravem ac meritis, fi forte virum quem
Confpexere, filent, adrectifque auribus adftant :

Æn. I.

full

full of confidence in God, he faces down the barbarian: the two Apoftles defcend not with the air of flaughtering angels, but (if facred may be compared with profane) like Jove, whofe very nod fhakes Olympus.

Algardi, in his celebrated reprefentation of the fame ftory, done in bas-relief on an altar in St. Peter's church at Rome, was either too negligent, or too weak, to give this active tranquillity of his great prede-ceffor to the figures of his Apoftles. There they appear like meffengers of the Lord of Hofts: here like human warriors with mortal arms.

How few of thofe we call connoiffeurs have ever been able to underftand, and fin-cerely to admire, the grandeur of expreffion in the St. *Michael* of *Guido*, in the church of the Capuchins at Rome! they prefer commonly the Archangel of *Concha*, whofe face glows with indignation and revenge[m];

whereas

m Vide Wright's Travels.
The victorious St. Michael of Guido, treads on
the

whereas *Guido*'s Angel, after having over-thrown the fiend of God and man, hovers over him unruffled and undifmayed.

Thus, to heighten the hero of *The Campaign*, victorious Marlborough, the Britifh poet paints the avenging Angel hovering over Britannia with the like ferenity and awful calmnefs.

The royal gallery at Drefden contains now, among its treafures, one of *Raphael*'s beft pictures, witnefs Vafari, &c. a Madonna with the Infant; St. Sixtus and St. Barbara kneeling, one on each fide, and two Angels in the fore-part.

It was the chief altar-piece in the cloifter of St. Sixtus at Piacenza, which was crouded by connoiffeurs, who came to fee this Raphael, in the fame manner as Thefpis was in the days of old, for the fake of the beautiful Cupid of *Praxiteles*.

the body of his antagonift, with all the precifion of a dancing-mafter. Webb's Inquiry, &c.

Be-

Behold the Madonna! her face brightens with innocence; a form above the female fize, and the calmnefs of her mien, make her appear as already beatified: fhe has that filent awfulnefs which the ancients fpread over their deities. How grand, how noble is her Contour!

The child in her arms is elevated above vulgar children, by a face darting the beams of divinity through every fmiling feature of harmlefs childhood.

St. Barbara kneels, with adoring ftillnefs, at her fide: but being far beneath the majefty of the chief figure, the great artift compenfated her humbler graces with foft enticing charms.

The Saint oppofite to her is venerable with age. His features feem to bear witnefs of his facred youth.

The veneration which St. Barbara declares for the Madonna, exprefled in the moft fenfible and pathetic manner, by her fine hands clafped on her breaft, helps to fupport

port the motion of one of St. Sixtus's hands, by which he utters his extafy, better becoming (as the artift judicioufly thought, and chofe for variety's fake) manly ftrength, than female modefty.

Time, 'tis true, has withered the primitive fplendour of this picture, and partly blown off its lively colours; but ftill the foul, with which the painter infpired his godlike work, breathes life through all its parts.

Let thofe that approach this, and the reft of *Raphael's* works, in hopes of finding there the trifling Dutch and Flemifh beauties, the laboured nicety of *Netfcher*, or *Douw*, flefh *ivorified* by *Van der Werf*, or even the licked manner of fome of *Raphael's* living countrymen; let thofe, I fay, be told, that *Raphael* was not a great mafter for them.

V. Workmanship in Sculpture.

AFTER these remarks on the Nature, the Contour, the Drapery, the simplicity and grandeur of Expression in the performances of the Greek artists, we shall proceed to some inquiries into their method of working.

Their models were generally made of wax ; instead of which the moderns used clay, or such like unctuous stuff, as seeming fitter for expressing flesh, than the more gluey and tenacious wax.

A method however not new, though more frequent in our times : for we know even the name of that ancient who first attempted modelling in wet clay ; 'twas *Dibutades* of Sicyon ; and *Arcesilaus*, the friend of *Lucullus*, grew more famous by his models of clay than his other performances. He made for *Lucullus* a figure of clay representing *Happiness*, and received 60,000 sesterces :

2

and

and *Octavius*, a Roman Knight, paid him a talent for the model only of a large dish, in plaifter, which he defigned to have finished in gold.

Of all materials, clay might be allowed to be the fitteft for fhaping figures, could it preferve its moiftnefs; but lofing that by time or fire, its folider parts, contracting by degrees, leffen the bulk of the mafs; and that which is formed, being of different diameters, grows fooner dry in fome parts than in others, and the dry ones being fhrunk to a fmaller fize, there will be no proportion kept in the whole.

From this inconvenience wax is always free: it lofes nothing of its bulk; and there are alfo means to give it the fmoothnefs of flefh, which is refufed to modelling; viz. you make your model of clay, mould it with plaifter, and caft the wax over it.

But for transferring their models to the marble, the Greeks feem to have poffeffed

fome

some peculiar advantages, which are now loft: for you difcover, every where in their works, the traces of a confident hand ; and even in thofe of inferior rank, it would be no eafy matter to prove a wrong cut.   Surely hands fo fteady, fo fecure; muft of neceffity have been guided by rules more determinate and lefs arbitrary than we can boaft of.

The ufual method of our fculptors is, to quarter the well-prepared model with horizontals and perpendiculars, and, as is common in copying a picture, to draw a relative number of fquares on the marble.

Thus, regular gradations of a fcale being fuppofed, every fmall fquare of the model has its correfponding one on the marble. But the contents of the relative maffes not being determinable by a meafured furface, the artift, though he gives to his ftone the refemblance of the model, yet, as he only depends on the precarious aid of his eye, he fhall never ceafe wavering, as to his doing right or wrong, cutting too flat or too deep.

Nor

Nor can he find lines to determine pre-
cifely the outlines, or the Contour of the
inward parts, and the centre of his model,
in fo fixed and unchangeable a manner, as
to enable him, exactly, to transfer the fame
Contours upon his ftone.

To all this add, that, if his work happens to be too voluminous for one fingle
hand, he muft truft to thofe of his journey-
men and difciples, who, too often, are neither fkilful nor cautious enough to follow
their mafter's defign; and if once the fmalleft
trifle be cut wrong, for it is impoffible to
fix, by this method, the limits of the cuts,
all is loft.

It is to be remarked in general, that
every fculptor, who carries on his chiffelings
their whole length, on firft fafhioning his
marble, and does not prepare them by gra-
dual cuts for the laft final ftrokes; it is to
be remarked, I fay, that he never can keep
his work free from faults.

Another

Another chief defect in that method is this : the artift cannot help cutting off, every moment, the lines on his block ; and though he reftore them, cannot poffibly be fure of avoiding miftakes.

On account of this unavoidable uncertainty, the artifts found themfelves obliged to contrive another method, and that which the French academy at Rome firft made ufe of for copying antiques, was applied by many even to modelled performances.

Over the ftatue which you want to copy, you fix a well-proportioned fquare, dividing it into equally diftant degrees, by plummets : by thefe the outlines of the figure are more diftinctly marked than they could poffibly be by means of the former method : they moreover afford the artift an exact meafure of the more prominent or lower parts, by the degrees in which thefe parts are near them, and in fhort, allow him to go on with more confidence.

But

But the undulations of a curve being not determinable by a fingle perpendicular, the Contours of the figure are but indifferently indicated to the artift; and among their many declinations from a ftraight furface, his tenour is every moment loft.

The difficulty of difcovering the real proportions of the figures, may alfo be eafily imagined: they feek them by horizontals placed acrofs the plummets. But the rays reflected from the figure through the fquares, will ftrike the eye in enlarged angles, and confequently appear bigger, in proportion as they are high or low to the point of view.

Neverthelefs, as the ancient monuments muft be moft cautioufly dealt with, plummets are ftill of ufe in copying them, as no furer or eafier method has been difcovered: but for performances to be done from models they are unfit for want of precifion.

Michael Angelo went alone a way unknown before him, and (ftrange to tell!) untrod

untrod fince the time of that genius of modern fculpture.

This Phidias of latter times, and next to the Greeks, hath, in all probability, hit the very mark of his great mafters. We know at leaft no method fo eminently proper for expreffing on the block every even the minuteft, beauty of the model.

Vafari [n] feems to give but a defective defcription of this method, viz. *Michael*

---

[n] Vafari vite de Pittori, Scult. et Arch. edit. 1568. Part III. p. 776.——" Quattro prigioni bozzati,
" che poffano infegnare à cavare de' Marmi le figure
" con un modo ficuro da non iftorpiare i faffi, che
" il modo è quefto, che s' e' fi pigliaffi una figura di
" cera ò d' altra materia dura, e fi meteffi à giacere
" in una conca d' acqua, la quale acqua effendo per
" la fua natura nella fua fommità piana et pari, al-
" zando la detta figura à poco del pari, cofi ven-
" gono à fcoprirfi prima le parti piu relevate e à
" nafconderfi i fondi, cioè le parti piu baffe della
" figura, tanto che nel fine ella cofi viene fcoperta
" tutta. Nel medefimo modo fi debbono cavare con
" lo fcarpello le figure de' Marmi, prima fcoprendo
" le parti piu rilevate, e di mano in mano le piu baffe,
" il quale modo fi vede offervato da Michael Angelo
" ne' fopra detti prigioni, i quali fua Eccellenza
" vuole, che fervino per efempio de fuoi Academici."

Angelo

Angelo took a veffel filled with water, in which he placed his model of wax, or fome fuch indiffoluble matter: then, by degrees, raifed it to the furface of the water. In this manner the prominent parts were unwet, the lower covered, 'till the whole at length appeared. Thus fays *Vafari*, he cut his marble, proceeding from the more prominent parts to the lower ones.

Vafari, it feems, either miftook fomething in the management of his friend, or by the negligence of his account gives us room to imagine it fomewhat different from what he relates.

The form of the veffel is not determined; to raife the figure from below would prove too troublefome, and prefuppofes much more than this hiftorian had a mind to inform us of.

Michael Angelo, no doubt, thoroughly examined his invention, its conveniencies and inconveniencies, and in all probability obferved the following method.

2   He

He took a veffel proportioned to his model; for inftance, an oblong fquare: he
marked the furface of its fides with certain
dimenfions, and thefe he transferred afterwards, with regular gradations, on the marble. The infide of the veffel he marked
to the bottom with degrees. Then he laid,
or, if of wax, faftened his model in it; he
drew, perhaps, a bar over the veffel fuitable
to its dimenfions, according to whofe number he drew, firft, lines on his marble, and
immediately after, the figure; he poured water on the model till it reached its outmoft
points, and after having fixed upon a prominent part, he drew off as much water as
hindred him from feeing it, and then went
to work with his chiffel, the degrees fhewing him how to go on; if, at the fame time,
fome other part of the model appeared, it
was copied too, as far as feen.

Water was again carried off, in order to
let the lower parts appear; by the degrees
he faw to what pitch it was reduced, and
by

by its fmoothnefs he difcovered the exact
furfaces of the lower parts ; nor could he go
wrong, having the fame number of degrees
to guide him, upon his marble.

The water not only pointed him out the
heights or depths, but alfo the Contour of
his model ; and the fpace left free on the
infides to the furface of the water, whofe
largenefs was determined by the degrees of
the two other fides, was the exact meafure
of what might fafely be cut down from the
block.

His work had now got the firft form, and
a correct one : the levelnefs of the water
had drawn a line, of which every prominence of the mafs was a point ; according
to the diminution of the water the line funk
in a horizontal direction, and was followed by
the artift 'till he difcovered the declinations
of the prominences, and their mingling with
the lower parts. Proceeding thus with every
degree, as it appeared, he finifhed the Contour, and took his model out of the water.

E

His

His figure wanted beauty : he again poured water to a proper height over his model,
and then numbering the degrees to the line
defcribed by the water, he defcried the exact height of the protuberant parts ; on thefe
he levelled his rule, and took the meafure
of the diftance, from its verge to the bottom ; and then comparing all he had done
with his marble, and finding the fame number of degrees, he was geometrically fure of
fuccefs.

Repeating his tafk, he attempted to exprefs the motion and re-action of nerves and
mufcles, the foft undulations of the fmaller
parts, and every imitable beauty of his model.   The water infinuating itfelf, even into
the moft inacceffible parts, traced their Contour with the correcteft fharpnefs and precifion.

This method admits of every poffible
pofture.   In profile efpecially, it difcovers
every inadvertency ; fhews the Contour of
    1   the

the prominent and lower parts, and the whole diameter.

All this, and the hope of fuccefs, pre-fuppofes a model formed by fkilful hands, in the true tafte of antiquity.

This is the way by which *Michael Angelo* arrived at immortality. Fame and rewards confpired to procure him what leifure he wanted, for performances which required fo much care.

But the artift of our days, however endowed by nature and induftry with talents to raife himfelf, and even though he perceive precifion and truth in this method, is forced to exert his abilities for getting bread rather than honour : he of courfe refts in his ufual fphere, and continues to truft in an eye directed by years and practice.

Now this eye, by the obfervations of which he is chiefly ruled, being at laft, though by a great deal of uncertain practice, become almoft decifive : how refined, how exact

E 2

might

might it not have been, if, from early youth, acquainted with never-changing rules !

And were young artifts, at their firft beginning to fhape the clay or form the wax, fo happy as to be inftructed in this fure method of *Michael Angelo*, which was the fruit of long refearches, they might with reafon hope to come as near the Greeks as he did.

VI. PAINTING.

GREEK Painting perhaps would fhare all the praifes beftowed on their Sculpture, had time and the barbarity of mankind allowed us to be decifive on that point.

All the Greek painters are allowed is Contour and Expreffion. Perfpective, Compofition, and Colouring, are denied them ; a judgment founded on fome bas-reliefs, and the new-difcovered ancient (for we dare not fay Greek) pictures, at and near Rome, in the fubterranean vaults of the palaces of

Mæcenas,

Mæcenas, Titus, Trajan, and the Antonini; of which but about thirty are preferved entire, fome being only in Mofaic.

Turnbull, to his treatife on ancient painting, has fubjoined a collection of the moft known ancient pictures, drawn by *Camillo Paderni,* and engraved by *Mynde*; and thefe alone give fome value to the magnificent and abufed paper of his work. Two of them are copied from originals in the cabinet of the late Dr. *Mead.*

That *Pouffin* much ftudied the pretended *Aldrovandine* Nuptials; that drawings are found done by *Annibal Carracci,* from the prefumed *Marcius Coriolanus*; and that there is a moft ftriking refemblance between the heads of *Guido,* and thofe on the Mofaic reprefenting *Jupiter* carrying off *Europa,* are remarks long fince made.

Indeed, if ancient Painting were to be judged by thefe, and fuch like remains of *Frefco* pictures, Contour and Expreffion might be wrefted from it in the fame manner.

For

For the pictures, with figures as big as life, pulled off with the walls of the Hercula-nean theatre, afford but a very poor idea of the Contour and Expreſſion of the ancient painters.   Theſeus, the conqueror of the Minotaur, worſhipped by the Athenian youths; Flora with Hercules and a Faunus; the pretended judgment of the Decemvir Appius Claudius, are on the teſtimony of an artiſt who ſaw them, of a Contour as mean as faulty; and the heads want not only Ex-preſſion, but thoſe in the Claudius even Character.

But even this is an evident inſtance of the meannels of the artiſts: for the ſcience of beautiful Proportions, of Contour, and Ex-preſſion, could not be the excluſive privilege of Greek ſculptors alone.

However, though I am for doing juſtice to the ancients, I have no intention to leſſen the merit of the moderns.

In Perſpective there is no compariſon be-tween them and the ancients, whom no
learned

earned defence can intitle to any fuperiority in that fcience. The laws of Compofition and Ordonnance feem to have been but imperfectly known by the ancients: the reliefs of the times when the Greek arts were flourifhing at Rome, are inftances of this. The accounts of the ancient writers, and the remains of Painting are likewife, in point of Colouring, decifive in favour of the moderns.

There are feveral other objects of Painting which, in modern times, have attained greater perfection: fuch are landfcapes and cattle pieces. The ancients feem not to have been acquainted with the handfomer varieties of different animals in different climes, if we may conclude from the horfe of M. Aurelius; the two horfes in Monte Cavallo; the pretended Lyfippean horfes above the portal of St. Mark's church at Venice; the Farnefian bull, and other animals of that groupe.

E 4

I ob-

I obferve, by the bye, that the ancients were carelefs of giving to their horfes the diametrical motion of their legs; as we fee in the horfes at Venice, and the ancient coins: and in that they have been followed, nay even defended, by fome ignorant moderns.

'Tis chiefly to oil-painting that our landfcapes, and efpecially thofe of the Dutch, owe their beauties: by that their colours acquired more ftrength and livelinefs; and even nature herfelf feems to have given them a thicker, moifter atmofphere, as an advantage to this branch of the art.

⸱ Thefe, and fome other advantages over the ancients, deferve to be fet forth with more folid arguments than we have hitherto had.

VII. ALLEGORY.

THERE is one other important ftep left towards the atchievement of the art: but the artift, who, boldly forfaking the

the common path, dares to attempt it, finds himfelf at once on the brink of a precipice, and ftarts back difmayed.

The ftories of martyrs and faints, fables and metamorphofes, are almoft the only objects of modern painters—repeated a thoufand times, and varied almoft beyond the limits of poffibility, every tolerable judge grows fick at them.

The judicious artift falls afleep over a Daphne and Apollo, a Proferpine carried off by Pluto, an Europa, &c. he wifhes for occafions to fhew himfelf a poet, to produce fignificant images, to paint Allegory.

Painting goes beyond the fenfes: *there* is its moft elevated pitch, to which the Greeks ftrove to raife themfelves, as their writings evince. Parrhafius, like Ariftides, a painter of the foul, was able to exprefs the character even of a whole people: he painted the Athenians as mild as cruel, as fickle as fteady, as brave as timid. Such a reprefentation owes its poffibility only to the allegorical

I

legorical method, whofe images convey general ideas.

But here the artift is loft in a defart.
Tongues the moft favage, which are entirely
deftitute of abftracted ideas, containing no
word whofe fenfe could exprefs memory,
fpace, duration, &c. thefe tongues, I fay,
are not more deftitute of general figns,
than painting in our days. The painter
who thinks beyond his palette longs for
fome learned apparatus, by whofe ftores he
might be enabled to inveft abftracted ideas
with fenfible and meaning images. Nothing
has yet been publifhed of this kind, to
fatisfy a rational being; the effays hitherto
made are not confiderable, and far beneath
this great defign. The artift himfelf knows
beft in what degree he is fatisfied with
Ripa's Iconology, and the emblems of ancient nations, by Van Hooghe.

Hence the greateft artifts have chofen but
vulgar objects. *Annibal Caracci,* inftead of
reprefenting in general fymbols and fenfible
images

images the hiftory of the Farnefian family, as an allegorical poet, wafted all his fkill in fables known to the whole world.

Go, vifit the galleries of monarchs, and the publick repofitories of art, and fee what difference there is between the number of allegorical, poetical, or even hiftorical performances, and that of fables, faints, or madonnas.

Among great artifts, *Rubens* is the moft eminent, who firft, like a fublime poet, dared to attempt this untrodden path. His moft voluminous compofition, the gallery of Luxembourg, has been communicated to the world by the hands of the beft engravers.

After him the fublimeft performance undertaken and finifhed, in that kind, is, no doubt, the cupola of the imperial library at Vienna, painted by *Daniel Gran*, and engraved by *Sedelmaycr*. The Apotheofis of Hercules at Verfailles, done by *Le Moine*, and alluding to the Cardinal *Hercules de Fleury*,

Fleury, though deemed in France the moft
auguft of compofitions, is, in comparifon of
the learned and ingenious performance of
the German artift, but a very mean and fhort-
fighted Allegory, refembling a panegyric, the
moft ftriking beauties of which are relative to
the almanack. The artift had it in his power
to indulge grandeur, and his flipping the
occafion is aftonifhing : but even allowing,
that the Apotheofis of a minifter was all
that he ought to have decked the chief
cieling of a royal palace with, we neverthelefs fee through his fig-leaf.

The artift would require a work, containing
every image with which any abftracted idea
might be poetically invefted : a work collected
from all mythology, the beft poets of all
ages, the myfterious philofophy of different
nations, the monuments of the ancients on
gems, coins, utenfils, &c. This magazine
fhould be diftributed into feveral claffes, and,
with proper applications to peculiar poffible
cafes, adapted to the inftruction of the artift.
                                                    This

This would, at the fame time, open a vaft field for imitating the ancients, and participating of their fublimer tafte.

The tafte in our decorations, which, fince the complaints of *Vitruvius*, hath changed for the worfe, partly by the grotefques brought in vogue by *Morte da Feltro*, partly by our trifling houfe-painting, might alfo, from more intimacy with the ancients, reap the advantages of reality and common fenfe.

The Caricatura-carvings, and favourite fhells, thofe chief fupports of our ornaments, are full as unnatural as the candlefticks of *Vitruvius*, with their little caftles and palaces : how eafy would it be, by the help of Allegory, to give fome learned convenience to the fmalleft ornament !

Reddere perfonæ fcit convenientia cuique.

Hor.

Paintings of ceilings, doors, and chimneypieces, are commonly but the expletives of thefe places, becaufe they cannot be gilt

all

all over,   Not only they have not the leaſt relation to the rank and circumſtances of the proprietor, but often throw ſome ridicule or reflection upon him.

'Tis an abhorrence of barenneſs that fills walls and rooms; and pictures void of thought muſt ſupply the vacuum.

Hence the artiſt, abandoned to the dictates of his own fancy, paints, for want of Allegory, perhaps a ſatire on him to whom he owes his induſtry; or, to ſhun this Charybdis, finds himſelf reduced to paint figures void of any meaning.

Nay, he may often find it difficult to meet even with thoſe, 'till at laſt

—— *velut ægri Somnia, vanæ*
Finguntur Species.   Hor.

Thus Painting is degraded from its moſt eminent prerogative, the repreſentation of inviſible, paſt and future things.

If pictures be ſometimes met with, which might be ſignificant in ſome particular
place,

place, they often lofe that property by ftupid and wrong applications.

Perhaps the mafter of fome new building

Dives agris, dives pofitis in fœnore nummis Hor.

may, without the leaft compunction for offending the rules of perfpective, place figures of the fmalleft fize above the vaft doors of his apartments and falloons. I fpeak here of thofe ornaments which make part of the furniture; not of figures which are often, and for good reafons, fet up promifcuoufly in collections.

The decorations of architecture are often as ill-chofen. Arms and trophies deck a hunting-houfe as nonfenfically, as Ganymede and the eagle, Jupiter and Leda, figure it among the reliefs of the brazen gates of St. Peter's church at Rome.

Arts have a double aim: to delight and to inftruct. Hence the greateft landfcape-painters think, they have fulfilled but half

their

their tafk in drawing their pieces without figures.

Let the artift's pencil, like the pen of Ariftotle, be impregnated with reafon ; that, after having fatiated the eye, he may nourifh the mind : and this he may obtain by Allegory ; invefting, not hiding his ideas. Then, whether he chufe fome poetical object himfelf, or follow the dictates of others, he fhall be infpired by his art, fhall be fired with the flame brought down from heaven by Prometheus, fhall entertain the votary of art, and inftruct the mere lover of it.

A
LETTER,
CONTAINING

OBJECTIONS

AGAINST

The foregoing REFLEXIONS.

F

A

LETTER

CONTAINING

OBJECTIONS againft the foregoing
REFLEXIONS.

S I R,

AS you have written on the Greek arts
and artifts, I wifh you had made your
treatife as much the object of your caution
as the Greek artifts made their works;
which, before difmiffing them, they exhibited
to publick view, in order to be examined by
every body, and efpecially by competent judges
of the art. The trial was held during the
grand, chiefly the Olympian, games; and all
Greece was interefted on Ætion's producing
his picture of the nuptials of Alexander and
Roxana. You, Sir, wanted a Proxenidas

F 2

to

to be judged by, as well as that artift; and had it not been for your myfterious concealment, I might have communicated your treatife, before its publication, to fome learned men and connoiffeurs of my acquaintance, without mentioning the author's name.

One of them vifited Italy twice, where he devoted all his time to a moft anxious examination of painting, and particularly feveral months to each eminent picture, at the very place where it was painted; the only method, you know, to form a connoiffeur. The judgment of a man able to tell you which of Guido's altar-pieces is painted on taffeta, or linnen, what fort of wood Raphael chofe for his transfiguration, &c. the judgment of fuch a man, I fancy, muft be allowed to be decifive.

Another of my acquaintance has ftudied antiquity: he knows it by the very fmell;

Callet & Artificem folo deprendere Odore.

Sectan. Sat.

He

He can tell you the number of knots on Hercules's club; has reduced Neftor's goblet to the modern meafure: nay, is fufpected of meditating folutions to all the queftions propofed by Tiberius to the grammarians.

A third, for feveral years paft, has neglected every thing but hunting after ancient coins. Many a new difcovery we owe to him; efpecially fome concerning the hiftory of the ancient coiners; and, as I am told, he is to roufe the attention of the world by a Prodromus concerning the coiners of Cyzicum.

What a number of reproaches might you have efcaped, had you fubmitted your Effay to the judgment of thefe gentlemen! they were pleafed to acquaint me with their objections, and I fhould be forry, for your honour, to fee them publifhed.

Among other objections, the firft is furprized at your paffing by the two Angels, in your defcription of the Raphael in the royal cabinet at Drefden; having been told, that a Bolognefe painter, in mentioning this piece,

which

which he faw at St. Sixtus's at Piacenza, breaks into thefe terms of admiration: O ! what Angels of Paradife[a] ! by which he fuppofes thofe Angels to be the moft beautiful figures of the picture.

The fame perfon would reproach you for having defcribed that picture in the manner of Raguenet[b].

The fecond concludes the beard of Laocoon to be as worthy of your attention as his contracted belly : for every admirer of Greek works, fays he, muft pay the fame refpect to the beard of Laocoon, which father Labat paid to that of the Mofes of Michael Angelo.

This learned Dominican,

Qui mores hominum multorum vidit & urbes,

has, after fo many centuries, drawn from

---

[a] Lettere d'alcuni Bologuefi, Vol. I. p. 159.

[b] Compare a defcription of a St. Sebaftian of Beccafumi, another of a Hercules and Antæus of Lanfranc, &c. in Raguenet's Monumens de Rome. Paris, 12mo.

this

this very ftatue an evident proof of the true
fafhion in which Mofes wore his own individual beard, and whofe imitation muft, of
courfe, be the diftinguifhing mark of every
true Jew[c].

There is not the leaft fpark of learning,
fays he, in your remarks on the Peplon of
the three veftals : he might perhaps, on the
very inflection of the veil, have difcovered
to you as many curiofities as Cuper himfelf
found on the edge of the veil of Tragedy
in the Apotheofis of Homer[d].

We alfo want proof of the veftals being

[c] Labat voyage en Efpagne & en Ital. T. III. p. 213.
——" Michel Ange étoit auffi favant dans l'antiquité
" que dans l'anatomie, la fculpture, la peinture, et
" l'architecture ; et puifqu' il nous a reprefenté Moyfe
" avec une fi belle et fi longue barbe, il eft fûr, et
" doit paffer pour conftant, que le prophete la por-
" toit ainfi ; et par une confequence neceffaire les
" Juifs, qui pretendent le copier avec exactitude, et
" qui font la plus grande partie de leur religion de
" l'obfervance des ufages qu' il a laiffé, doivent avoir
" de la barbe comme lui, ou renoncer à la qualité
" de Juifs."
[d] Apotheof. Homeri, p. 81, 82.

F 4
really

really Greek performances : our reafon fails
us too often in the moft obvious things.   If
unhappily the marble of thefe figures fhould
be proved to be no Lychnites, they are loft,
and your treatife too: had you but flightly
told us their marble was large-grained, that
would have been a fufficient proof of their
authenticity ; for it would be fomewhat difficult to determine the bignefs of the grains
with fuch exactnefs as to diftinguifh the
Greek marble from the Roman of Luna.
But the worft is, they are even denied the
title of veftals.

The third mentioned fome heads of Livia
and Agrippina, without that pretended profile of yours.   Here he thinks you had the
moft lucky occafion to talk of that kind of
nofe by the ancients called *Quadrata*, as an
ingredient of beauty.   But you no doubt
know, that the nofes of fome of the moft
famous Greek ftatues, viz. the Medicean
Venus, and the Picchinian Meleager, are
                                                    much

much too thick for becoming the model of beauty, in that kind, to our artifts.

I fhall not, however, gall you with all the doubts and objections raifed againft your treatife, and repeated to naufeoufnefs, upon the arrival of an Academician, the Margites of our days, who, being fhewed your treatife, gave it a flight glance, then laid it afide, offended as it were at firft fight. But it was eafy to perceive that he wanted his opinion to be afked, which we accordingly all did. " The author, faid he very peremptorily, feems not to have been at much pains with this treatife : I cannot find above four or five quotations, and thofe negligently inferted; no chapter, no page, cited ; he certainly collected his remarks from books which he is afhamed to produce."

Yet cannot I help introducing another gentleman, fharp-fighted enough to pick out fomething that had efcaped all my attention; viz. that the Greeks were the

firft

first inventors of Painting and Sculpture; an affertion, as he was pleafed to exprefs himfelf, entirely falfe, having been told it was the Egyptians, or fome people ftill more ancient, and unknown to him.

Even the moft whimfical humour may be turned to profit: neverthelefs, I think it manifeft that you intended to talk only of good Tafte in thofe arts; and the firft Elements of an art have the fame proportion to good Tafte in it, as the feed has to the fruit. That the art was ftill in its infancy among the Egyptians, when it had attained the higheft degree of perfection among the Greeks, may be feen by examining one fingle gem: you need only confider the head of *Ptolomæus Philopator* by Aulus, and the two figures adjoining to it done by an Egyptian [e], in order to be convinced of the little merit this nation could pretend to in point of art.

[e] Stofch Pierr. Grav. pl. **XIX.**

The

The form and taſte of their Painting have been aſcertained by Middleton. ' The pictures of perſons as big as life, on two mummies in the royal cabinet of antiquities at Dreſden, are evident inſtances of their incapacity. But theſe relicks being curious, in ſeveral other reſpects, I ſhall hereafter ſubjoin a ſhort account of them.

I cannot, my friend, help allowing ſome reaſon for ſeveral of theſe objections. Your negligence in your quotations was, no doubt, ſomewhat prejudicial to your authenticity : the art of changing blue eyes to black ones, certainly deſerved an authority. You imitate Democritus ; who being aſked, " What is man ?" every body knows what was his reply. What reaſonable creature will ſubmit to read all Greek ſcholiaſts !

Ibit eo, quo vis, qui Zonam perdidit—
Hor.

Conſidering, however, how eaſily the hu-

' Monum. Antiquit. p. 255.

man

man mind is biaffed, either by friendfhip or animofity, I took occafion from thefe objections to examine your treatife with more exactnefs ; and fhall now, by the moft impartial cenfure, ftrive to clear myfelf from every imputation of prepoffeffion in your favour.

I will pafs by the firft and fecond page, though fomething might be faid on your comparifon of the Diana with the Nauficaa, and the application : nor would it have been amifs, had you thrown fome more light on the remark concerning the mifufed pictures of Corregio (very likely borrowed from Count Teffin's letters), by giving an account of the other indignities which the pictures of the beft artifts, at the fame time, met with at Stockholm.

It is well known that, after the furrender of Prague to Count Konigfmark, the 15th of July 1648, the moft precious pictures of the Emperor Rodolph II. were carried off

to

to Sweden [g]. Among these were some pictures of Corregio, which the Emperor had been presented with by their first possessor, Duke Frederick of Mantua; two of them being the famous Leda, and a Cupid handling his bow [h]. Christina, endowed at that time rather with scholastic learning than taste, treated these treasures as the Emperor Claudius did an Alexander of Apelles; who ordered the head to be cut off, and that of Augustus to fill its place [i]. In the same manner heads, hands, feet were here cut off from the most beautiful pictures; a carpet was plastered over with them, and the mangled pieces fitted up with new heads, &c. Those that fortunately escaped the common havock, among which were the pieces of Corregio, came afterwards, together with several other pictures, bought by

[g] Puffendorf Rer. Suec. L. XX. §. 50. p. 796.
[h] Sandrart Acad. P. II. L. 2. c. 6. p. 118. Conf. St. Gelais descr. des Tabl. du Palais Royal, p. 12. & seq.
[i] Plin. Hist. Nat. L. 35. c. 10.

the Queen at Rome, into the poſſeſſion of
the Duke of Orleans, who purchaſed 250
of them, and among thoſe eleven of Corregio, for 9000 Roman crowns.

But I am not contented with your charg-
ing only the northern countries with bar-
bariſm, on account of the little eſteem they
paid to the arts.   If good taſte is to be judged
in this manner, I am afraid for our French
neighbours.   For having taken Bonn, the
reſidence of the Elector of Cologne, after
the death of Max. Henry, they ordered the
largeſt pictures to be cut out of their frames,
without diſtinction, in order to ſerve for coverings to the waggons, in which the moſt
valuable furniture of the electoral caſtle was
carried off for France.   But, Sir, do not
preſume on my continuing with mere hiſtorical remarks : I ſhall proceed with my objections; after making the two following general obſervations.

I. You have written in a ſtÿle too conciſe for being diſtinct.   Were you afraid of
being

being condemned to the penalty of a Spartan, who could not reftrain himfelf to only three words, perhaps that of reading Picciardin's Pifan War? Diftinctnefs is required where univerfal inftruction is the end. Meats are to fuit the tafte of the guefts, rather than that of the cooks,

—— Cœnæ fercula noftræ
Malim convivis quam placuiffe coquis.

II. There appears, in almoft every line of yours, the moft paffionate attachment to antiquity; which perhaps I fhall convince you of, by the following remarks.

The firft particular objection I have to make is againft your third page. Remember, however, that my paffing by two pages is very generous dealing:

non temere a me
Quivis ferret idem: Hor.

but let us now begin a formal trial.

The

The author talks of certain negligences in the Greek works, which ought to be confidered fuitably to Lucian's precepts concerning the Zeus of Phidias: " Zeus himfelf, not his footftool;" [k] though perhaps he could not be charged with any fault in the foot-ftool, but with a very grievous one in the ftatue.

Is it no fault that Phidias made his *Zeus* of fo enormous a bulk, as almoft to reach the cieling of the temple, which muft infallibly have been thrown down, had the god taken it in his head to rife? [l] To have left the temple without any cieling at all, like that of the Olympian Jupiter at Athens, had been an inftance of more judgment [m].

'Tis but juftice to claim an explication of what the author means by " negligences". He perhaps might be pleafed to get a paff-port, even for the faults of the ancients, by fheltering them under the authority of

[k] Lucian de Hift. Scrib.
[l] Strabo Geogr. L. VIII. p. 542.
[m] Vitruv. L. III. c. 1.

fuch

such titles; nay, to change them into beauties, as Alcæus did the spot on the finger of his beloved boy. We too often view the blemishes of the ancients, as a parent does those of his children:

Strabonem
Appellat pætum pater, & pullum, male parvus
Si cui filius est.   Hor.

If these negligences were like those wished for in the Jalysus of Protogenes, where the chief figure was out-shone by a partridge, they might be considered as the agreeable negligée of a fine lady; but this is the question. Besides, had the author consulted his interest, he never would have ventured citing the Diomedes of Dioscorides: but being too well acquainted with that gem, one of the most valued, most finished monuments of Greek art; and being apprehensive of the prejudice that might arise against the meaner productions of the ancients, on discovering many faults in one so eminent as Diomedes;

G   he

he endeavoured to keep matters from being too nearly examined, and to soften every fault into negligence.

How! if by argument I shall attempt to shew that Diofcorides underftood neither perfpective, nor the moft trivial rules of the motion of a human body; nay, that he offended even againft poffibility? I'll venture to do it, though

> *incedo per ignes*
> *Suppofitos cineri dolofo.*   Hor.

And perhaps I am not the firft difcoverer of his faults: yet I do not remember to have feen any thing relative to them.

The Diomedes of Diofcorides is either a fitting, or a rifing figure; for the attitude is ambiguous. It is plain he is not fitting; and rifing is inconfiftent with his action.

Our body endeavouring to raife itfelf from a feat, moves always mechanically towards its fought-for centre of gravity, drawing back the

the legs, which were advanced in fitting[n]; inftead of which the figure ftretches out his right leg. Every erection begins with elevated heels, and in that moment all the weight of the body is fupported only by the toes, which was obferved by Felix[o], in his Diomedes: but here all refts on the fole.

Nor can Diomedes, (if we fuppofe him to be a fitting figure, as he touches with his left leg the bottom of his thigh) find, in raifing himfelf, the centre of his gravity, only by a retraction of his legs, and of courfe cannot rife in that pofture. His left hand refting upon the bended leg, holds the palladion, whilft his right touches negligently the pedeftal with the point of a fhort fword; confequently he cannot rife, neither moving his legs in the natural and eafy manner required in any erection, nor making

[n] Borell. de motu animal. P. I. c. 18. prop. 142. p. 142. edit. Bernouc.

[o] Stofch. Pierr. Grav. pl. XXXV.

G 2 ufe

ufe of his arms to deliver himfelf from that uneafy fituation.

There is at the fame time a fault committed againft the rules of perfpective.

The foot of the left bended leg, touching the cornice of the pedeftal, fhews it over-reaching that part of the floor, on which the pedeftal and the right foot are fituated, confequently the line defcribed by the hinder-foot is the fore on the gem, and *vice verfa*.

But allowing even a poffibility to that fituation, it is contrary to the Greek character, which is always diftinguifhed by the natural and eafy. Attributes neither to be met with in the contorfions of Diomedes, nor in an attitude, the impoffibility of which every one muft be fenfible of, in endeavouring to put himfelf in it, without the help of former fitting.

Felix, fuppofed to have lived after Diofcorides, though preferving the fame attitude, has endeavoured to make its violence more natural, by oppofing to him the figure of

Ulyffes,

Ulyſſes, who, as we are told, in order to bereave him of the honour of having ſeized the Palladion, offered to rob him of it, but being diſcovered, was repulſed by Diomedes; which being his ſuppoſed action on the gem, allows violence of attitude [P].

Diomedes cannot be a ſitting figure, for the Contour of his buttock and thigh is free, and not in the leaſt compreſſed: the foot of the bent leg is viſible, and the leg itſelf not bent enough.

The Diomedes repreſented by Mariette is abſurd; the left leg reſembling a claſped pocket-knife, and the foot being drawn up ſo high as to make it impoſſible in nature that it ſhould reach the pedeſtal [q].

Faults of this kind cannot be called neg-ligences, and would not be forgiven in any modern artiſt.

Dioſcorides, 'tis true, in this renowned performance did but copy Polycletus, whoſe

[P] Stoſch Pierr. Grav. pl. XXXV.
[q] Mariette Pierr. Grav. T. II. n. 94.

G 3 Dorypho-

Doryphorus (as is commonly agreed) was the beſt rule of human proportions[r]. But, though a copyiſt, Dioſcorides eſcaped a fault which his maſter fell into. For the pedeſtal, over which the Diomedes of Polycletus ſeans, is contrary to the moſt common rules of perſpective ; its cornices, which ſhould be parallel, forming two different lines.

I wonder at Perrault's omitting to make objections againſt the ancient gems.

I mean not to do any thing derogatory to the author, when I trace ſome of his particular obſervations to their ſource.

The food preſcribed to the young wreſtlers, in the remoter times of Greece, is mentioned by Pauſanias[s]. But if the author alluded to the paſſage which I have in view, why does he talk in general of milk-food, when Pauſanias particularly mentions ſoft cheeſe ?

[r] Stoſch Pierr. Grav. pl. LIV.
[s] Pauſanias, L. VI. c. 7. p. 470.

Dromeus

Dromeus of Stymphilos, we learn there, firft introduced flefh meat.

My refearches, concerning their myfterious art of changing blue eyes to black ones, have not fucceeded to my wifh. I find it mentioned but once, and that only by the bye by Diofcorides[t]. The author, by clearing up this art, might perhaps have thrown a greater luftre over his treatife, than by producing his new method of ftatuary. He had it in his power to fix the eyes of the Newtons and Algarotti's, on a problem worth their attention, and to engage the fair fex, by a difcovery fo advantageous to their charms, efpecially in Germany, where, contrary to Greece, large, fine, blue eyes are more frequently met with than black ones.

There was a time when the fafhion required to be green eyed:

> *Et fi bel oeil vert & riant & clair :*
> Le Sire de Coucy, chanf.

[t] Diofcorid. de Re Medica, L. V. c. 179. Conf. Salmaf. Exercit. Plin. c. 15. p. 134. b.

But

But I do not know whether art had any
ſhare in their colouring. And as to the ſmall-
pox, Hippocrates might be quoted, if gram-
matical diſquiſitions ſuited my purpoſe.

However, I think, no effects of the ſmall-
pox on a face can be ſo much the reverſe of
beauty, as that defect which the Athenians were
reproachfully charged with, viz. a buttock as
pitiful as their face was perfect[u]. Indeed
Nature, in ſo ſcantily ſupplying thoſe parts,
ſeemed to derogate as much from the Athenian beauty, as, by her laviſhneſs, from that
of the Indian Enotocets, whoſe ears, we
are told, were large enough to ſerve them
for pillows.

As for opportunities to ſtudy the nudities,
our times, I think, afford as advantageous
ones as the Gymnaſies of the ancients.
'Tis the fault of our artiſts to make no
uſe of that[w] propoſed to the Pariſian artiſts,

[u] Ariſtoph. Nub. v. 1178. ibid. v. 1363. Et Scho-
liaſt.

[w] Obſervat. ſur les arts, ſur quelques morceaux de
peint. & ſculpt. expoſés au Louvre en 1748. p. 18.

viz.

viz. to walk, during the fummer feafon, along the Seine, in order to have a full view of the naked parts, from the fixth to the fiftieth year.

'Tis perhaps to Michael Angelo's frequenting fuch opportunities that we owe his celelebrated Carton of the Pifan war [x], where the foldiers bathing in a river, at the found of a trumpet leap out of the water, and make hafte to huddle on their cloaths.

One of the moft offenfive paffages of the treatife is, no doubt, the unjuft debafement of the modern fculptors beneath the ancients. Thefe latter times are poffeffed of feveral Glycons in mufcular heroic figures, and, in tender youthful female bodies, of more than one Praxiteles. *Michael Angelo, Algardi,* and *Sluter,* whofe genius embellifhed Berlin, produced mufcular bodies,

—— *Invicti membra Glyconis,*

Hor.

[x] Ripofo di Raffaello Borghini, L. I. p. 46.

in

in a ſtyle rivalling that of Glycon himſelf;
and in delicacy the Greeks are perhaps even
outdone by *Bernini, Fiammingo, Le Gros,
Rauchmüller, Donner.*

The unſkilfulneſs of the ancients, in
ſhaping children, is agreed upon by our artiſts, who, I ſuppoſe, would for imitation
chooſe a Cupid of Fiammingo rather than
of Praxiteles himſelf. The ſtory of M. Angelo's placing a Cupid of his own by the ſide
of an antique one, in order to inform our
times of the ſuperiority of the ancient art, is
of no weight here : for no work of Michael
Angelo can bring us ſo near perfection as
Nature herſelf.

I think it no hyperbole to advance, that
Fiammingo, like a new Prometheus, produced creatures which art had never ſeen
before him. For, if from almoſt all
the children on ancient gems [y] and re-

---

[y] See the Cupid by Solon, Stoſch. 64. the Cupid
leading the Lioneſs, by Sostratus, Stoſch. 66. and
a Child and Faun, by Axeochus, Stoſch 20.

             liefs

liefs [z], we may form a conclusion of the art itself, it wanted the true expression of childhood, as loofer forms, more milkinefs, and unknit bones. Faults which, from the epoch of Raphael, all children laboured under, till the appearance of *Francis Quefnoy*, called Fiammingo, whofe children having the advantages of fuitable innocence and nature, became models to the following artifts, as in youthful bodies Apollo and Antinous are: an honour which *Algardi*, his contemporary, may be allowed to fhare.

Their models in clay are, by our artifts, efteemed fuperior to all the antique marble children; and an artift of genius and talents affured me, that during a ftay of feven years at Vienna, he faw not one copy taken from an ancient Cupid in that academy.

Neither do I know on what fingular idea of beauty, the ancient artifts founded their cuftom, of hiding the foreheads of their

[z] Vide Bartoli Admiranda Rom. fol. 50, 51. 61. Zanetti Stat. Antich. P. II. fol. 33.

children

children and youths with hair.   Thus a
Cupid was reprefented by Praxiteles[a]; thus
a Patroclus, in a picture mentioned by Phi-
loftratus[b]: and there is no ftatue nor buft,
no gem nor coin of Antinous, in which we
do not find him thus dreffed.   Hence, perhaps, that gloom, that melancholy, with
which all the heads of this favourite of Hadrian are marked.

Is not there in a free open brow more
noblenefs and fublimity ? and does not
Bernini feem to have been better acquainted
with beauty than the ancients, when he re-
moved the over-fhadowing locks from the
forehead of young Lewis XIV. whofe buft
he was then executing ? " Your Majefty,
faid Bernini, is King, and may with confidence fhew your brow to all the world."
From that time King and court dreffed their
hair à la Bernini[c].

---

[a] Vide Calliftrat. p. 903.
[b] Vide Philoftrati Heroic.
[c] Vide Baldinucci vita del Caval. Bernin. p. 47.

His

His judgment of the bas-reliefs on the monument of Pope Alexander VI [d]. leads us to some remarks on those of antiquity. " The skill in bas-relief, said he, consists in giving the air of relief to the flat : the figures of that monument seem what they are indeed, not what they are not."

The chief end of bas-relief is to deck those places that want hiftorical or allegorical ornaments, but which have neither cornices fufficiently fpacious, nor proportions regular enough to allow groupes of entire ftatues : and as the cornice itfelf is chiefly intended to fhelter the fubordinate parts from being directly or indirectly hurt, no bas-relief muft exceed the projection thereof ; which would not only make the cornice of no ufe, but endanger the figures themfelves.

The figures of ancient bas-reliefs fhoot commonly fo much forward as to become almoft round. But bas-relief being founded

[d] Vide Baldinucci vita del Caval. Bernin. p. 72.

on

on fiction, can only counterfeit reality; its perfection is well to imitate; and a natural maſs is againſt its nature if flat, ought to appear projected, and *vice verſa*. If this be true, it muſt of courſe be allowed that figures wholly round are inconſiſtent with it, and are to be conſidered as ſolid marble pillars built upon the theatre, whoſe aim is mere illuſion; for art, as is ſaid of tragedy, wins truth from fiction, and that by truth. To art we often owe charms ſuperior to thoſe of nature: a real garden and vegetating trees, on the ſtage, do not affect us ſo agreeably, as when well expreſſed by the imitating art. A roſe of *Van Huiſum,* mallows of *Veerendal,* bewitch us more than all the darlings of the moſt ſkilful gardener: the moſt enticing landſcape, nay, even the charms of the Theſſalian Tempe, would not, perhaps, affect us with that irreſiſtible delight which, flowing from *Dietrick's* pencil, enchants our ſenſes and imagination.

By

By fuch inftances we may fafely form a judgment of the ancient bas-reliefs: the royal cabinet at Drefden is poffeffed of two eminent ones: a Bacchanal on a tomb, and a facrifice to Priapus on a large marble vafe.

The bas-relief claims a particular kind of fculpture; a method that few have fucceeded in, of which *Matielli* may be an inftance. The Emperor Charles VI. having ordered fome models to be prepared by the moft renowned artifts, in bas-relief, intended for the fpiral columns at the church of S. Charles Borromæo; *Matielli*, already famous, was principally thought of; but however refufed the honour of fo confiderable a work, on account of the enormous bulk of his model, which requiring too great cavities, would have diminifhed the mafs of the ftone, and of courfe weakened the pillars. *Mader* was the artift, whofe models were univerfally applauded, and who by his admirable execution proved that he deferved

that

that preference. Thefe bas-reliefs reprefent the ftory of the patron of this church.

It is in general to be obferved, firft, that this kind of fculpture admits not indifferently of every attitude and action; as for inftance, of too ftrong projections of the legs. Secondly, That, befides difpofing of the feveral modelled figures in well-ranged groupes, the diameter of every one ought to be applied to the bas-relief itfelf, by a leffened fcale: as for inftance, the diameter of a figure in the model being one foot, the profile of the fame, according to its fize, will be three inches, or lefs: the rounder a figure of that diameter, the greater the fkill. Commonly the relief wants perfpective, and thence arife moft of its faults.

Though I propofed to make only a few remarks on the ancient bas-relief, I find myfelf, like a certain ancient Rhetor, almoft under a neceffity of being new-tuned. I have ftrayed beyond my limits; though at the fame time I remembered that there is a law.

law among commentators, to content themfelves with bare remarks on the contents of a
treatife: and alfo fenfible that I am writing
a letter, not a book, I confider that I may
draw fome inftructions for my own ufe,

—— *ut vineta egomet cædam mea,*

Hor.

from fome people's impetuofity againft the
author; who, becaufe they are hired for it,
feem to think that writing is confined to
them alone.

The Romans, though they worfhipped
the deity Terminus (the guardian God of limits and borders in general; and, if it pleafe
thefe gentlemen, of the limits in arts and
fciences too), allowed neverthelefs an univerfal unreftrained criticifm: and the de-
cifions of fome Greeks and Romans, in
matters of an art, which they did not
practife, feem neverthelefs authentick to our
artifts.

H   Nor

Nor can I find, that the keeper of the temple of peace at Rome, though poffeffed of the regifter of the pictures there, pretended to monopolize remarks and criticifms upon them; Pliny having defcribed moft of them.

Publica materies privati juris fit—

Hor.

'Tis to be wifhed, that, roufed by a Pamphilus and an Apelles, artifts would take up the pen themfelves, in order to difcover the myfteries of the art to thofe that know how to ufe them,

Ma di coftor', che à lavorar s' accingono,
Quattro quinti, per Dio, non fanno leggere.
Salvator Rofa, Sat. III.

Two or three of thefe are to be commended; the reft contented themfelves with giving fome hiftorical accounts of the fraternity. But what could appear more aufpicious to the improvement of the art, even

by

by the remoteſt poſterity, than the work
attempted by the united forces of the celebrated Pietro da Cortona [e] and Padre Otto-
nelli ? Neverthelefs this fame treatife, except
only a few hiſtorical remarks, and thefe too
to be met with in an hundred books, feems
good for nothing, but

Ne ſcombris tunicæ deſint, piperique cuculli.

Sectan. Sat.

How trivial, how mean are the great
Pouſſin's reflexions on painting, publiſhed
by Bellori, and annexed to his life of that
artiſt [f] ?

Another digreſſion !—let me now again
refume the character of your Ariſtarchus.

You are bold enough to attack the authority of *Bernini*, and to challenge a
man, the bare mention of whofe name
would do honour to any treatife. It was

---

[e] Trattato della pittura e fcultura, ufo et abufo
loro, compofto da un theologo e da un pittore. Fio-
renza, 1652. 4.

[f] Bellori vite de 'pittori, &c. p. 300.

Ber-

Bernini, you ought to recollect, Sir, who at the fame age in which Michael Angelo performed his *Studiolo*[g], viz. in his eighteenth year, produced his Daphne, as a convincing inftance of his intimacy with the ancients, at an age in which perhaps the genius of Raphael was yet labouring under darknefs and ignorance!

Bernini was one of thofe favourites of nature, who produce at the fame time vernal bloffoms and autumnal fruits; and I think it by no means probable, that his ftudying nature in riper years mifled either him or his difciples. The fmoothnefs of his flefh was the refult of that ftudy, and imparted to the marble the higheft poffible degree of life and beauty. Indeed 'tis nature which endows art with life, and " vivifies forms," as Socrates fays[h], and Clito the fculptor allows. The great Lyfippus, when afked

[g] Richardfon, Tom. III. p. 94.
[h] Xenophon Memorab. L. III. c. 6, 7.

which

which of his anceftors he had chofen for his mafter, replied, " None; but nature alone." It is not to be denied, that the too clofe imitation of antiquity is very often apt to lead us to a certain barrennefs, unknown to thofe who imitate nature: various her-felf, nature teaches variety, and no votary of her's can be charged with a famenefs: whereas Guido, Le Brun, and fome other votaries of antiquity, repeated the fame face in many of their works. A certain ideal beauty was become fo familiar to them, as to flide into their figures even againft their will.

But as for fuch an imitation of nature, as is quite regardlefs of antiquity, I am entirely of the author's opinion; though I fhould have chofen other artifts as inftances of following nature in painting.

Jordans certainly has not met with the re-gard due to his merit; let me appeal to an authority univerfally allowed. " There is,

" fays

" says Mr. d'Argenville, more expreſſion and
" truth in Jordans, than even in Rubens.

   " Truth is the baſis and origin of per-
" fection and beauty; nothing, of any kind
" whatever, can be beautiful or perfect,
" without being truly what it ought to be,
" without having all it ought to have."

   The ſolidity of this judgment preſup-
poſed, *Jordans*, according to Rochefoucault's
maxims, ought rather to be ranked among
the greateſt originals, than among the mimicks of common nature, where *Rembrandt*
may fill up his place, as *Raoux* or *Vatteau*
that of *Stella*; though all theſe painters do
nothing but what Euripides did before them;
they draw man *ad vivum*. There are no
trifles, no meanneſſes in the art, and if we
recollect of what uſe the *Caricatura* was to
Bernini, we ſhould be cautious how we
paſs judgment even on the Dutch forms.
That great genius, they ſay [1], owed to this

---

[1] Vide Baldinucci vita del Cav. Bernini, p. 66.

monſter

monfter of the art, a diftinction for which
he was fo eminent, the " Franchezza del
Tocco." When I reflect on this, I am forced
to alter my former opinion of the *Carica-*
tura, fo far as to believe that no artift ever
acquired a perfection therein without gaining
a farther improvement in the art itfelf. " It
is, fays the author, a peculiar diftinction of
the ancients to have gone beyond nature :"
our artifts do the fame in their *Caricaturas :*
but of what avail to them are the voluminous
works they have publifhed on that branch
of the art ?

The author lays it down, in the pe-
remptory ftyle of a legiflator, that " Precifion of Contour can only be learned from
the Greeks :" but our academies unanimoufly agree, that the ancients deviate from
a ftrict Contour in the clavicles, arms, knees,
&c. over which, in fpite of apophyfes and
bones, they drew their fkin as fmooth as
over mere flefh; whereas our academies
teach to draw the bony and cartilaginous

H 4   parts,

parts, more angularly, but the fat and flefhy ones more fmooth, and carefully to avoid falling into the ancient ftyle. Pray, Sir, can there be any error in the advices of academies *in corpore?*

Parrhafius himfelf, the father of Contour, was not, by Pliny's account [k], mafter enough to hit the line by which completenefs is diftinguifhed from fuperfluity: fhunning corpulency he fell into leannefs: and *Zeuxis*'s Contour was perhaps like that of Rubens, if it be true that, to augment the majefty of his figures, he drew with more completenefs. His female figures he drew like thofe of Homer [l], of robuft limbs: and does not even the tendereft of poets, Theocritus, draw his Helen as flefhy and tall [m] as the Venus of Raphael in the affembly of the gods in the little Farnefe? Rubens then, for painting like Homer and Theocritus, needs no apology.

[k] Plin. Hift. Nat. L. 35. c. 10.
[l] Quintilian. Inftit. Or. L. 12. c. 19.
[m] Idyll. 18. v. 29.

The

The character of Raphael, in the treatise, is drawn with truth and exactness: but well may we aſk the author, as Antalcidas the Spartan aſked a ſophiſt, ready to burſt forth in a panegyrick on Hercules, " Who blames him ?" The beauties however of the Raphael at Dreſden, eſpecially the pretended ones of the Jeſus, are ſtill warmly diſputed.

> *What you admire, we laugh at.*
>   Lucian, Ep. I.

Why did not he rather diſplay his patriotiſm againſt thoſe Italian connoiſſeurs, whoſe ſqueamiſh ſtomachs riſe againſt every Flemiſh production ?

> *Turpis Romano Belgicus ore color.*
>   Propert. L. II. Eleg. 8.

And indeed are not colours ſo eſſential, that without them no picture can aſpire to univerſal applauſe ? Do not their bewitching charms cover the moſt grievous faults? They are the harmonious melody of painting ;
                                        what-

whatever is offensive vanishes by their splendor, and souls animated with their beauties are absorbed in beholding, as the readers of Homer are by his flowing harmony, so as to find no faults. These, joined to that important science of Chiaro-Oscuro, are the characteristicks of Flemish painting.

Agreeably to affect our eye is the first thing in a picture [a], which to obtain, obvious charms are wanted; not such as spring only from reflection. Colouring moreover belongs peculiarly to pictures; whereas design ought to be in every draught, print, &c. and indeed seems easier to be attained than colouring.

The best colourists, according to a celebrated writer [o], have always come *after* the inventors and contourists; we all know the vain attempts of the famous Poussin. In short, all those

[a] De Pile's Conversat. sur la peint.
[o] Du Bos Refl. sur la poesie & sur la peint.

Qui

Qui rem Romanam Latiumque augefcere
 ftudent,   Ennius.

muft here acknowledge the fuperiority of the Flemifh art; the painter being really but nature's mimick, is the more perfect the better he mimicks her.

Aft heic, quem nunc tu tam turpiter
 increpuifti,   Ennius.

the delicate *Van der Werf,* whofe perform-ances, worth their weight in gold, are the ornaments of royal cabinets only, has made nature inimitable to every Italian pencil; he allures the connoiffeur's eye as well as that of the clown; and, as an Englifh poet fays, " that no pleafing poet ever wrote ill," furely the Flemifh painter obtained that ap-plaufe which was denied to Pouffin.

  I fhould be glad to fee many pictures as happily fancied, as well compofed, as en-ticingly painted as fome of *Gherard Laireffe:* let me appeal to every unprepoffeffed artift

            at

at Paris, acquainted with the *Stratonice*,
the moſt eminent, and no doubt the firſt
ranked picture in the cabinet of Mr. de la
Boixieres ᴾ.

The ſubject is of no trivial choice : King
Seleucus I. ꝗ reſigned his wife Stratonice, a
daughter of Demetrius Poliorcetes, to his ſon
Antiochus, whom a violent paſſion for his
mother-in-law had thrown into a dangerous
ſickneſs : after many unſucceſsful inquiries,
the phyſician Eraſiſtratus diſcovered the true
cauſe, and found that the only means of
reſtoring the prince's health, was, the condeſcenſion of the father to the love of his
ſon : the King reſigned his Queen, and at
the ſame time declared Antiochus King of
the Eaſt.

ᴾ The Stratonice was twice painted by Laireſſe.
The picture we talk of is the ſmalleſt of the two : the
figure is about one foot and a half, and differs from
the other in the diſpoſition of the Parerga.

ꝗ See Plutarch. in Demetr. & Lucian. de Dea
Syria.

Stratonice,

Stratonice, the chief perfon, is the nobleft figure, a figure worthy Raphael himfelf. The charming Queen,

Colle fob idæo vincere digna deas,

Ovid. Art.

with flow and hefitating fteps, approaches the bed of her new lover; but ftill with the countenance of a mother, or rather of a facred veftal. In the profile of her face you may read fhame mingled with gentle refignation to the will of her lord. She has the foftnefs of her fex, the majefty of a queen, an awful fubmiffion to the facred ceremony, and all the fagenefs required in fo extraordinary and delicate a fituation. Dreffed with a mafterly fkill, the artift, from the colour of her cloaths, may learn how to paint the purple of the ancients; for it is not generally known that it refembled fadeing, ruddy, vine-leaves [r].

[r] Vide Lettre de Mr. Huet fur la Pourpre: dans les Differtat. de Tilladet. Tom. II. p. 169.

Behind

I

Behind her ſtands the King, dreſſed in a darker habit, in order to give the more re-lief to the Queen, to ſpare confuſion to her, ſhame to the Prince, and not to interrupt his joy. Expectation and acquieſcence are blended in his face, which is taken from the profile of his beſt coins.

The Prince, a beautiful half-naked youth, ſitting in his bed, has ſome reſemblance of his father; his pale face bears witneſs of the fever, that lately had raged in his veins; but fancy ſees returning health, not ſhame, in that ſoft-riſing ruddineſs diffuſed over his cheeks.

The phyſician and prieſt Eraſiſtratus, ve-nerable like the Calchas of Homer, ſtand-ing before the bed, is the only ſpeaker, au-thoriſed by the King, whoſe will he declares to the Prince; and whilſt, with one hand, he leads the Queen to the embraces of her lover, with the other he preſents him with the diadem. Joy and aſtoniſhment flaſh

from

from the Prince's face on the approach of his Queen

—— darting all the foul in miſſive love:

though nobly reſtrained by reverence, he bends his head, and ſeems to compriſe his happineſs in a ſingle thought.

The characters indeed are diſtributed with ſo much ingenuity, that they ſeem to give a luſtre and energy to each other.

The largeſt ſhare of light is diſplayed on Stratonice: ſhe claims our firſt regard. The prieſt, though in a weaker light, is raiſed by his geſture: he is the ſpeaker, and around him reign ſolemn ſtillneſs and attention.

The Prince, the ſecond perſon, has a larger ſhare of light; and though the artiſt, led by his ſkill, choſe rather to make a beautiful Queen the chief ſupport of his groupe than a ſick Prince, He nevertheleſs maintains his due rank, and becomes the moſt eminent perſon of the whole, by his expreſ-

expreffion. His face contains the greateft
fecrets of the art,

Quales nequeo monftrare & fentio tantum.
                              Juvenal. Sat. VII.

Even thofe motions of the foul, which
otherwife feem oppofite to each other,
mingle here with peaceful harmony; a
timid red fpreading over his fickly face, an-
nounces health, like the faint glimmerings
of the morn, which, though veiled by night,
announce the day, and even a bright one.

The genius and tafte of the artift fhines
forth in every part of his work: even the
vafes are copied from the beft antique ones;
the table before the bed, is, like Homer's, of
ivory.

The diftances behind the figures reprefent a magnificent Greek building, whofe
decorations feem allegorical. The roof of
a portal is fupported by Cariatides embracing
each other, as images of the tender friend-
                                        fhip

fhip between father and fon, and alluding, at the fame time, to the nuptial cere-. mony.

Though faithful to hiftory, the painter was neverthelefs a poet: in order to reprefent fome circumftances, he filled even the furniture with fentiments. The Sphinxes by the Prince's bed allude to his problematic ficknefs, the enquiries of Erafiftratus, and his fagacity in difcovering its true caufe.

I have been told that fome young Italian artifts, when confidering this picture, and perceiving the Prince's arm perhaps a trifle too big, went off without enquiring into the fubject itfelf. Should even Minerva herfelf, as fhe once did to Diomedes, attempt to deliver fome people from the mift they labour under, by heaven! the attempt were vain!

> —— *pauci dignofcere poffunt*
> *Vera bona, atque illis multum diverfa, remota*
> *Erroris nebula.*
>
> Juv. X.

I have

I have run into this long digreffion, in order to throw fome light on one of the firft productions of the art, which is neverthe-lefs but little known.

The idea of noble fimplicity and fedate grandeur in Raphael's figures, might rather, as two eminent authors exprefs it[1], be called " ftill life." It is indeed the ftandard of the Greek art: however, indifcreetly commended to young artifts, it might beget as dangerous confequences, as precepts of energetick con-cifenefs in the ftyle; the direct method to make it barren and unpleafing.

" In youths, fays Cicero[2], there muft
" be fome fuperfluity, fomething to be taken
" off: prematurity fpoils the juices, and it
" is eafier to lop the young rank branches of
" a vine, than to reftore its vigour to a
" worn out trunk." Not to mention, that figures wanting gefture would, by the bulk

[1] St. Real Cæfarion, T. II. Le Blanc Lettre fur l'Expof. des Ouvrages de Peint, &c. 1747.
[2] De Oratore, L. II. c. 21.

of

of mankind, be received as a fpeech before the Areopagites, where, by a fevere law, the fpeaker was forbid to raife any paffions, though ever fo gentle [u]: nay, pictures of this kind would be fo many portraits of young Spartans, who, with hands hid under their coats, and down-caft eyes, ftalk forth in filent folemnity [w].

Neither am I quite of the author's opinion with regard to allegory; the applying of which would too frequently do in painting, what was done in geometry by introducing algebra: the one would foon be as difficult as the other, and painting would degenerate into Hieroglyphicks.

The author attempts, in vain, to perfuade us, that the majority of the Greeks thought as the Egyptians. There was no more learning in the painting of the platfond of the temple of Juno at Samos, than in that of the Farnefe gallery. It reprefented the love-

[u] Arif̃tot. Rhet. L. I. c. 1. §. 4.
[w] Xenophon Refp. Laced. c. 3. §. 5.

I 2   intrigues

intrigues of Jupiter and Juno[x]: and, in the front of a temple of Ceres at Eleufis, there was nothing but reprefentations of a ceremony at the rites of that goddefs[y].

How to reprefent abftract ideas I do not yet diftinctly conceive. There may be the fame difficulties which attend the endeavours of reprefenting to the fenfes a mathematical point—perhaps nothing lefs than impoffibility; and Theodoretus[z] has fome reafon in confining painting to the fenfes. For thofe Hieroglyphicks which hint at abftract ideas, in fuch a manner as to exprefs, for inftance[a], *youth* by the number XVI; *impoffibility* by two feet ftanding on water: thofe, I fay, are monograms, not images: to indulge them in painting is foftering chimæras, is

[x] Origines Contra Celf. L. IV. p. 196. Edit. Cantabr.

[y] Perrault fur Vitruve Explic. de la Planche IX. p. 62.

[z] Dialog. Inconfuf. p. 76.

[a] Horapoll. Hierogl. c. 33. Conf. Blackwell's Enq. into Hom. p. 170.

adding

adding to Chinese pictures Chinese explications.

An adversary of allegory believes that Parrhasius, without any help from it, could represent the contradictions in the character of the Athenians; that he did it perhaps in several pictures. Supposing which

*Et sapit, & mecum facit, & Jove judicat
aequo.* Hor.

The sentence of death pronounced against the leaders of the Athenian navy, after their victory over the Spartans near the Arginuses, afforded the artist a very sensible and rich image, to represent the Athenians, at the same time, merciful and cruel.

The famous Theramenes, one of the leaders, accused his fellow-chieftains of having neglected to gather and bury the bodies of their slain countrymen: a charge sufficient to rouse the rage of the mob against the victors; only six of whom had returned to Athens, the rest having declined the storm.

I 3 Thera-

Theramenes harangued the people in the moft pathetick manner; intermixing his fpeech with frequent paufes, in order to give vent to the loud plaints of thofe who, in the battle, had loft their parents or relations. He, at the fame time, produced a man, who protefted he had heard the laft words of the drowned, imprecating the publick revenge on their leaders. In vain did Socrates, then a member of the council, with a few others, oppofe the accufation: the brave chieftains, inftead of the honours they hoped for, were condemned to die. One of them was the only fon of *Pericles* and *Afpafia.*

Was it not in the power of Parrhafius, who was then alive, to enlarge the meaning of his picture beyond the extent of bare hiftory, only by drawing the true characters of the authors of this fcene, without the leaft help from allegory? It would have been in his power, had he lived in our days.

Your

Your pretenfions concerning allegory feem indeed as reafonable an impofition upon the painter, as that of Columella upon his farmer; who wifhed to find him a philofopher like Democritus, Pythagoras, or Eudoxus [b].

No better fuccefs, in my opinion, is to be expected from applying allegory to decorations : the author would, at leaft, meet with as many difficulties as Virgil, when hammering on the names of a Vibius Caudex, Tanaquil Lucumo, or Decius Mus, to fit them for his Hexameter.

Cuftom has given its fanction to the ufe of fhells in decorations : and is not there as much nature in them as in the Corinthian capital ? You know its origin : a bafket fet upon the tomb of a young Corinthian girl, filled with fome of her play-things, and covered with a large brick, being overgrown

[b] De Re ruft. præf. ad L. I. §. 32. p. 392. Edit. Gefn.

I 4

with

with the creeping branches of an acanthus, which had taken root under it, was the firſt occaſion of forming that capital. *Callimachus* [c] the ſculptor, ſurprized at the elegant ſimplicity of that compoſition, took thence a hint for enriching architecture with a new order.

Thus this capital, deſtined to ſupport all the entablature of the column, is but a baſket of flowers; ſomething ſo apparently inconſiſtent with the ideas of architecture, that there was no uſe made of it in the time of Pericles: for Pocock [d] thinks it ſtrange that the temple of Minerva at Athens had Doric, inſtead of Corinthian pillars. But time ſoon changed this ſeeming oddity into nature; the baſket loſt, by cuſtom, all its former offenſiveneſs, and

Quod fuerat vitium definit eſſe mora.

Ovid. Art.

[c] Vitruv. L. IV. c. I.
[d] Travels, T. II.

We

We acknowledge no Egyptian law to forbid arbitrary ornaments; and fo fond have the artifts of all ages been, both of the growth and form of fhells, as to change even the chariot of Venus into an enormous one. The ancile, that Palladium of the Romans, was fcooped into the form of a fhell[e]: we find them on antique lamps[f]. Nay, nature herfelf feems to have produced their immenfe variety, and marvellous finuations, for the benefit of the art.

I have no mind to plead the bad caufe of our unfkilful decorators: only let me adduce the arguments ufed by a whole tribe, (if the artifts will forgive the term), in order to prove the reafonablenefs of their art.

The painters and fculptors of Paris, endeavouring to deprive the decorators of the title of artifts, by alledging that they employed neither their own intellectual facul-

[e] Plutarch. Numa, p. 149. L. 14. Edit. Bryani.
[f] Pafferii Lucern.

ties,

ties, nor thofe of the connoiffeurs, upon works not produced by nature, but rather the offsprings of capricious art; the others are faid to have defended themfelves in the following manner: " We are the followers " of nature: like the bark of a tree, vari- " oufly carved, our decorations grow into " various forms: then art joins fportive na- " ture, and corrects her: we do what the " ancients did: confult their decorations."

Variety is the great and only rule to which decorators fubmit. Perceiving that there is no perfect refemblance between two things in nature, they likewife forfake it in their decorations; and carelefs of anxious twining, leave it to the parts themfelves to find their like, as the atoms of Epicurus did. This liberty we owe to the very nation, which, after having nobly exceeded all the narrow bounds of focial formalities, beftows fo much pains upon communicating her improve- ments to her neighbours. This ftyle in de- corations got the epithet of *Barroque* tafte, derived

derived from a word fignifying pearls and teeth of unequal fize [g].

Shells have at leaft as good a claim for being admitted among our decorations, as the heads of fheep and oxen. You know that the ancients placed thofe heads, ftript of the fkin, on the frizes, efpecially of the Doric order, between the Triglyphs, or on the Metopes. We even meet with them on the Corinthian frife of an old temple of Vefta, at Tivoli [h]; on tombs, as on one of the Metellus-family near Rome, and another of Munatius Plancus near Gaeta [i]; on vafes, as on a pair in the royal cabinet at Drefden. Some modern artifts, finding them perhaps unbecoming, changed them into thunder-bolts, like Vignola, or to rofes, like Palladio and Scamozzi [k].

[g] Menage Diction. Etymol. v. Barroque.

[h] Vide Defgodez Edifices antiq. de **Rome,** p. 91.

[i] Bartoli Sepolcri Antichi, p. 67. **ibid.** fig. 91.

[k] Perrault notes fur Vitruv. L. IV. ch. 2. n. 21. p. 118.

We

We conlude from all this, that learning never had, nor indeed ought to have, any ſhare in an art ſo nearly related to what we call *Luſus Naturæ.*

Thus the ancients thought: for, pray, what could be meant by a lizard on Mentor's cup? [l]   The

Picti ſquallentia terga lacerti

Virg. G. IV.

make, to be ſure, a lovely image amidſt the flowers of a Rachel Ruyſch, but a very poor figure on a cup.   Of what myſterious meaning are birds picking grapes from vines, on an urn? [m]   Images, perhaps, as void of ſenſe, and as arbitrary, as the fable of Ganymede embroidered on the mantle, which Æneas preſented to Cloanthus, as a reward of his victory in the naval games [n].

[l] Martial, L. III. Ep. 41. 1.
[m] Bellori Sepolchri ant. f. 99.
[n] Virgil, Æn. V. v. 250. & ſeq.

To

To conclude: is there any thing contra-dictory between trophies and the hunting-houfe of a Prince? Surely the author, though fo zealous a champion for the Greek tafte, cannot pretend to propofe to us that of King Philip and the Macedonians, who, by the account of Paufanias °, did not erect their own trophies. Diana perhaps, amidft her nymphs and hunting-equipages,

> *Qualis in Eurotæ ripis, aut per juga*
> *Cynthi,*
> *Exercet Diana choros, quam mille fecutæ,*
> *Hinc atque hinc glomerantur, Oreades——*
> Virg.

might better fuit the place; but we know that the antient Romans hung up the arms of their defeated enemies over the out-fides of their doors, to be everlafting monitors of bravery to every fucceeding owner of the houfe. Can trophies, having the fame de-

---

° Paufanias, L. IX. c. 40. p. 794. Conf. Spanhem. Not. fur les Cæfars de l'Emp. Julien. p. 240.

fign,

fign, ever be mifplaced on any building of
the Great ?

I wifh for a fpeedy anfwer to this letter.
You cannot be angry at feeing it publifhed.
The tribe of authors now imitate the con-
duct of the ftage, where the lover, with his
foliloquy, entertains the pit.   For the fame
reafon I fhall receive, with all my heart, an
anfwer,

> *Quam legeret tereretque viritim publicus*
> *ufus :*   Hor.

for

> *Hanc veniam petimufque damufque vi-*
> *ciffim.*   Id.

A N

A N
ACCOUNT
OF A
MUMMY,

I N

The Royal Cabinet of Antiquities
at DRESDEN.

AN ACCOUNT

OF A

MUMMY,

IN

The Royal Cabinet of Antiquities
at DRESDEN.

AMONG the Egyptian Mummies of
the royal cabinet, there are two preferved perfectly entire, and not in the leaft
damaged, viz. the bodies of a man and
woman. The former, among all thofe
that were brought into, and publickly known
in Europe, is perhaps the only one of its
kind; on account of an infcription thereon,
which none of thofe who have written on
Mummies, except Della Valle alone, difco-

K · vered

vered on thofe bodies; and Kircher, among all the drawings of Mummies communi-cated to him, and publifhed in his Oedipus, has but one, (the fame which Della Valle had been poffeffed of,) with an infcription; though his wooden cut [a] is as faulty as all the copies made afterwards [b]. On that Mummy there are thefe letters EΥ✝ΥXI.

This fame infcription is on the royal Mummy, of which I propofe to give a brief account, and in examining which I have employed all my attention, that I might be certain of its being genuine, and not drawn by a modern hand from the infcription of Della Valle: for 'tis well known, that thofe bodies frequently pafs through the hands of Jews. But the letters are evidently drawn with the fame blackifh colour with which the face, hands, and feet are ftained. The firft letter on our Mummy has the form of

[a] Kircheri Oedip. Ægypt. T. III. p. 405, & 433.
[b] Bianchini Iftor. Univ. p. 412.

I

a large

a large Greek Є, expreſſed by Della Valle
with an E angular, the other not being
uſual in printing-preſſes.

All the four Mummies of the royal cabinet being bought at Rome, I propoſed to
examine whether the Mummy with the inſcription, was that which Della Valle was
poſſeſſed of, and found that both the entire
royal Mummies were exact reſemblances of
thoſe deſcribed by him.

Both, beſides the linnen bandages, of a
Barracan-texture, rolled innumerable times
around the bodies, are wrapt up in ſeveral
(and, according to an obſervation made in
England [c], in three) kinds of coarſer linnen ;
which, by particular bandages of the girdle-
kind, is faſtened in ſuch a manner as to in-
volve even the ſmalleſt prominence of the
face. The firſt covering is a nice bit of
linnen, ſlightly tinged with a certain ground,

[c] Nehem. Grew Muſæum Societ. Reg. Lond.
1681. fol. p. 1.

K 2   much

much gilt, decked with various figures, and with a painted one of the deceafed.

On the Mummy marked with the in-fcription, this figure reprefents a man, who died in the flower of life, with a thin curled beard, not as reprefented by Kircher, like an old man with a long pointed one. The colour of the face and hands is brown: the head encircled with gilt diadems, marked with the fockets of jewels. From the gold chain, painted around the neck, a fort of medal hangs down, marked with various charaçters, crefcents, &c. and this over-reaches the neck of a bird, that of a hawk perhaps, as on the breafts of other Mummies [d]. In the right hand of the figure is a difh filled with a red ftuff, which being like that ufed by the facrificers [e], the deceafed may be fuppofed to have been a prieft. The firft and laft finger of the left hand have rings; and in

[d] Vide Gabr. Bremond Viaggi nell'Egitto. Roma. 1579. 4. L. I. c. 15. p. 77.
[e] Clemens Alex. Strom. L. VI. p. 456.

the

the hand itfelf there is fomething round, of a dark-brown colour ; which, as Della Valle pretends, is a well-known fruit. The feet and legs are bare, with fandals ; the ftrings of which appearing between the great toes, are, with a flip, faftened on the foot itfelf.

The infcription, above-mentioned, is beneath the breaft.

The fecond Mummy is the ftill more refined figure of a young woman. Among a great many medals, feemingly gilt, and other figures, there are certain birds, and quadrupeds fomething analogous to lions ; and towards the extremities of the body there is an ox, perhaps an apis. Down from one of the neck-chains hangs a gilt image of the fun. She has ear-rings, and double bracelets on both her arms : rings on each hand, and on every finger of the left one, but two on the firft : whereas the right hand has but two : with this hand fhe holds, like Ifis, a fmall gilt veffel, of the Greek Spondeion-kind, which was a fymbol of the

K 3

ferti-

fertility of the Nile, when held by the goddefs [f]. In the left hand there is a fort of
fruit, like an ear of corn, of a greenifh caft.
The leaden feals, mentioned by Della Valle,
ftill remain on the firft Mummy.

Compare this defcription with that in his
travels [g], and you'll find the Mummies of
the royal cabinet to be the fame with thofe,
which were taken out of a deep well or
cave, covered with fand, and fold to this
celebrated traveller by an Egyptian; and I
believe they were purchafed from his heirs at
Rome, though in the manufcript catalogue,
joined to that cabinet of antiquities, there is
not the leaft hint of any fuch purchafe.

I have no defign to attempt an explication of the ornaments and figures; fome remarks of that kind having already been
made by Della Valle. The following obfervations concern only the infcription.

[f] Shaw, Voyage, T. II. p. 123.
[g] Della Valle Viaggi. Lettr. 11. §. 9. p. 325. &
feq.

The

. The Egyptians, we know, employed a double character in expreſſing themſelves [h]; the *ſacred* and the *vulgar :* the firſt was what is called hieroglyphick; the other contained the characters of their national language, and this is commonly ſaid to be loſt. All we know is confined to the twenty-five letters of their alphabet. [i] Della Valle ſeems inclined to give an inſtance of the contrary, in that inſcription; which Kircher, puſhing his conjectures ſtill farther, endeavours to lay down as a foundation for a new ſcheme of his, and to ſupport it by two other remains of the ſame kind. For, he attempts to prove [k], that the dialect was the only difference between the old Egyptian and Greek tongue. According to his talent of finding what no body looks for, he makes free with ſome ancient hiſtorical accounts; upon which he obtrudes a fictitious

[h] Herodot. L. II. c. 36. Diod. Sic.
[i] Plutarch. de Iſid. & Oſirid. p. 374.
[k] Kircher Oed. I. c. ej. Prodrom. Copt. c. 7.

ſenſe,

fenfe, in order to make them tally with his fcheme.

Herodotus, according to him, tells us, that King Pfammetichus defired fome Greeks, who were perfect mafters of their language, to go over to Egypt, in order to inftruct his people in the purity of the tongue. Hence he concludes, that there was but one language in both countries. But that Greek hiftorian [1] gives an account entirely oppofite: he tells us, that Pfammetichus, having received fome fervices from the Carians and Ionians, permitted them to fettle in Egypt, for the inftruction of youth in the Greek language, in order to bring up interpreters.

There is no folidity in the reft of the Kircherian arguments; fuch as thofe deduced from the frequent voyages of the Greek fages into Egypt, and the mutual commerce between the two nations; which have not even the ftrength of conjectures. For the

[1] Herodot. L. II. c. 153.

very

very skill of Democritus, in the sacred tongue of the Babylonians and Egyptians [m], proves only, that the travelling sages learned the languages of the nations they conversed with.

Nor does the testimony of Diodorus, that Attica was originally an Egyptian colony [n], seem to be here of any weight.

The inscription of the Mummy might indeed admit of Kircherian, or such like conjectures, were the Mummy itself of the antiquity pretended by Kircher. Cambyses, the conqueror of Egypt, partly exiled, and partly killed the priests; from which fact Kircher confidently deduces as consequences, the total abolition of the sacred rites, and from that the ceasing to embalm bodies. He again appeals to a passage of Herodotus [o], which, upon his word alone, others have as confidently quoted. Nay, a certain pedant

---

[m] Diogen. Laert. v. Democr.

[n] Diodor. Sic. L. I. c. 29. Edit. Wessel.

[o] Kircher Oedip I. c. — it. ejusd. China illustrata. III. c. 4. p. 151.

went

went fo far as to pretend, that the Egyptian cuftom of painting their dead, upon the varnifhed linnen of the Mummies, ceafed with the epoch of Cyrus [p].

But Herodotus fays not a word, either of the total abolition of the facred rites, or of the abolition of the cuftom of preferving the dead from putrefaction, after the time of Cambyfes; nor does Diodorus Siculus give any fuch hint: we may, on the contrary, from his account of the funeral rites of the Egyptians, rather conclude, that this cuftom prevailed even in his time; that is to fay, when Egypt was changed into a Roman province.

Hence it cannot be demonftrated that our Mummy was embalmed before the Perfian conqueft.----But fuppofing it to be of that date, is it a neceffary confequence that a body preferved in the Egyptian manner, or even taken care of by their priefts, fhould be marked with Egyptian words?

[p] Alberti Englifche Briefe, B——.

Perhaps

Perhaps it is the body of some naturalised Ionian or Carian. We know that Pythagoras entered into the Egyptian confession; nay, even consented to be circumcised [q], in order to shorten his way to the mysteries of their priests. The Carians themselves observed the sacred solemnities of Isis, and even went so far in their superstition, as to mangle their faces during the sacrifices offered to that deity [r].

Change the letter *ι*, in the inscription, into the diphthong *ει*, and you have a Greek word: such negligences are often to be met with in Greek marbles [s], and still more in Greek manuscripts; and with the same termination it is to be found on a gem, and signifies, "FAREWELL" [t], which was the usual ejaculation addressed by the living to the deceased; the same we meet with on ancient

[q] Clem. Alex. Strom. L. I. p. 354. Edit. Pott.
[r] Herodot. L. II. c. 61.
[s] Montfaucon Palæogr. Græc. L. III. c. 5. p. 230. Kuhn. Not. ad Pausan. L. II. p. 128.
[t] Augustin. Gem. P. II. l. 32.

epitaphs;

epitaphs"; public decrees"; and of letters
it was the final conclusion ˣ.

There is on an ancient epitaph the word
ΕΥΨΥΧΙ ʸ; the form of the Ψ on ancient
stones and manuscripts is exactly the same ᶻ
with the third letter of ΕΥ✝ΥΧΙ, which
was perhaps confounded with it.

But suppofing the Mummy to be of later
times, the adoption of a Greek word becomes yet eafier. The round form of the Є
might be fomething fufpicious, with regard to
its pretended antiquity; that form being never found on the gems or coins before Au-
guftus ᵃ. But this fufpicion becomes of no
weight, by suppofing that the Egyptians

ᵘ Gruter. Corp. Infcr. p. DCCCLXI. ἐυτυχεῖτε,
χαιρέτε, &c.

ʷ Prideaux Marm. Oxon. 4. & 179.

ˣ Demofth. Orat. pro Corona, p. 485. 499. Edit.
Frc. 1604.

ʸ Gruter Corp. Infcript. p. DCXLI. 8.

ᶻ Montfaucon Palæogr. L. IV. c. 10. p. 336.
338.

ᵃ Montf. L. I. c. 4. II. c. 6. p. 152.

I   conti-

continued their embalming, even after the time of that Emperor.

However, the word cannot be an Egyptian one, being inconfiftent with the remains of that ancient tongue in the modern Coptick, as well as with their manner of writing; which was from the right to the left, as the Etrurians did [b]; whereas the word in queftion (like fome Egyptian characters [c],) is traced from the left to the right. As for the infcription difcovered by Maillet [d], no interpreter has yet been found. The Grecians, on the contrary, wrote in the occidental manner, for fix hundred years before the chriftian æra, witnefs the Sigæan infcription, which is faid to be of that date [e].

What has been faid relates alfo to an

[b] Herod. L. II.

[c] Defcript. de l'Egypte, par Mafcriere, Lettr. VII. 23.

[d] Defcript. de l'Eg. L. c.

[e] Chifhul. Infcr. Sig. p. 12.

infcrip-

infcription upon a piece of ftone [f], with Egyptian figures, communicated to Kircher by Carolo Vintimiglia, a Palerman patrician. The letters ITIΨIXI are two words, and fignify, " *Let the foul come.*") This ftone has met with the fame fate as the gem engraved with the head of Ptolomæus Philopator : for here an Egyptian has joined two random figures, and there the infcription may be of a Greek hand. The litterati know what little change it wants to be orthographical.

[f] Kircher. Obelifc, Pamph. c. 8. p. 147.

AN

ANSWER

TO THE FOREGOING

LETTER,

AND

A further EXPLICATION of the
SUBJECT.

A N

A N S W E R

TO THE FOREGOING

L E T T E R,

A N D

A Further Explication of the Subject.

I COULD not prefume that fo fmall a treatife as mine would be thought of confequence enough to be brought to a publick trial. As it was written only for a few *connoiffeurs*, it feemed fuperfluous to give it a learned air, by multiplying quotations. Artifts want but hints: their tafk, according to an ancient Rhetor, is " to perform, not to perufe;" confequently every author, who writes for them, ought to be brief. Being beſides convinced, that the beauties of the art are founded rather on a quick ſenſe, and refined taſte, than on profound meditation, I cannot help thinking that the principle of Neoptolemus [a], " to philoſophize only with the few," ought to be the chief conſideration in every treatiſe of this kind.

Several paſſages of my Eſſay are ſuſceptible of explications, and, having been publickly tried by an anonymous author, ſhould be explained and defended at the ſame time, if my circumſtances would permit me to enlarge [b]. As to his other remarks, the author, I hope, will gueſs at my anſwer, without my giving one explicitly.—Indeed they do not require any.

I am not in the leaſt moved by the clamours concerning thoſe pieces of *Corregio*, which, by undoubted accounts, were not

_____

[a] Cicero de Oratore, L. II. c. 37.
[b] The author was then preparing for a journey to Rome.

only

only brought to *Sweden* [c], but even hung up in the ſtables at *Stockholm.* Reaſoning is of no uſe here: arguments of this kind admit of no other evidence but that of *Æmilius Scaurus* againſt *Valerius* of *Sucro:* " He denies; I affirm: Romans! 'tis yours to judge."

And why ſhould there be any thing more derogatory to the honour of the Swedes, in my repeating Count *Teſſin*'s relation, than in his giving it? Perhaps, becauſe the learned author of the circumſtantial life of Queen *Chriſtina* omits her indiſcreet generoſity towards *Bourdon*, and that bad treatment which the pictures of *Corregio* met with? or was *Härleman* [d] himſelf charged with indiſcretion or malice, on his relating that, at *Lincöping,* he found a college, and ſeven profeſſors, but not one phyſician or artificer?

---

[c] Argenville abregé de la V. d. P. T. II. p. 287.
[d] Reiſe, p. 21.

It

It was my deſign to explain myſelf more particularly, concerning the negligences of the Greeks, had I been allowed time. The Greeks, as their criticiſm on the partridge of Protogenes, and his blotting it [e], evidently ſhews, were not ignorant in learned negligence. But the Zeus of Phidias was the ſtandard of ſublimity, the ſymbol of the omnipreſent Deity; like Homer's Eris, he ſtood upon the earth, and reached heaven; he was, in the ſtyle of ſacred poeſy, " *What encompaſſes him?* &c." And the world has been candid enough to excuſe, nay, even to juſtify on ſuch reaſons, the diſproportions in the Carton of Raphael, repreſenting the fiſhing of Peter [f]. The criticiſm on the *Diomedes*, though ſolid, is not againſt me: his action, abſtractedly conſidered, with his noble and expreſſive contour, are ſtandards of the art; and that was all I advanced [g].

The

---

[e] Strabo, L. XIV. p. 652. al. 965. l. 11.

[f] Richardſon Eſſay, &c. p. 38, 39.

[g] Diomedes, for ought I can ſee, is neither a
fitting

The reflections on the Painting and Sculpture of the Greeks may be reduced to four heads, viz.

I. The perfect Nature of the Greeks;
II. The Characteristicks of their works;
III. The Imitation of these;
IV. Their manner of Thinking upon the Art; and Allegory.

Probability was all I pretended to, with regard to the first; which cannot be fully demonstrated, notwithstanding all the assistance of history. For, these advantages of the Greeks were, perhaps, less founded on their nature, and the influences of the climate, than on their education.

The happy situation of their country was, however, the basis of all; and the want of resemblance, which was observed between the Athenians and their neighbours beyond

fitting nor a standing figure, in both which cases the critick must be allowed to be just. He descends.
Remark of the T. L.

L 3   the

the mountains, was owing to the difference of air and nouriſhment [h].

The manners and perſons of the new-ſettled inhabitants, as well as the natives of every country, have never failed of being influenced by their different natures. The ancient Gauls, and their ſucceſſors the German Franks, are but one nation : the blind fury, by which the former were hurried on in their firſt attacks, proved as unſucceſsful to them in the times of Cæſar [i], as it did to the latter in our days. They poſſeſſed certain other qualities, which are ſtill in vogue among the modern French; and the Emperor Julian [k] tells us, that in his time there were more dancers than citizens at Paris.

Whereas the Spaniards, managing their affairs cautiouſly, and with a certain frigidity, kept the Romans longer than any

[h] Cicero de Fato, c. 4.
[i] Strabo, L. IV. p. 196. al. 299. l. 22.
[k] Miſopog. p. 342. l. 13.

other

other people from conquering the country [1].

And is not this character of the old Ibe-
rians re-affumed by the Weft-Goths, the
Mauritanians, and many other people, who
over-ran their country ? [m]

It is eafy to be imagined what advantages
the Greeks, having been fubject to the fame
influences of climate and air, muft have
reaped from the happy fituation of their
country. The moft temperate feafons reign-
ed through all the year, and the refrefhing
fea-gales fanned the voluptuous iflands of
the Ionick fea, and the fhores of the conti-
nent. Induced by thefe advantages, the
Peloponnefians built all their towns along
the coaft; fee Dicearchus, quoted by Cicero [n].

Under a fky fo temperate, nay balanced
between heat and cold, the inhabitants can-

---

[1] Strabo, L. III. p. 158. al. 238.
[m] Du Bos Reflex. fur la Poefie et f. l. P. II. 144.
[n] Herodot. L. III. c. 106. Cicero ad Attic. L. VI.
cp. 2.

not

not fail of being influenced by both. Fruits grow ripe and mellow, even ſuch as are wild improve their natures; animals thrive well, and breed more abundantly. "Such a ſky, ſays Hippocrates [o], produces not only the moſt beautiful of men, but harmony between their inclinations and ſhape." Of which Georgia, that country of beauty, where a pure and ſerene ſky pours fertility, is an inſtance [p]. Among the elements, beauty owes ſo much to water alone, that, if we believe the Indians, it cannot thrive, in a country that has it not in its purity [q]. And the Oracle itſelf attributes to the lymph of Arethuſa a power of forming beauty [r].

The Greek tongue affords us alſo ſome arguments in behalf of their frame. Na-

[o] Περὶ τοπων. p. 288. edit. Foeſii. Galenus ὅτι τα τῆς Ψυχῆς Ἤθη τοις του Σωματος κρασεσι ἑπέται. fol. 171. B. I. 43. edit. Ald. T. I.

[p] Chardin voyage en Perſe, T. II. p. 127. & ſeq.

[q] Journal des Sçavans l'An. 1684. Aur. p. 153.

[r] Apud Euſeb. Præpar. Evang. L. V. c. 29. p. 226. edit. Colon.

ture

ture moulds the organs of ſpeech according to the influences of the climate. There are nations that rather whiſtle than ſpeak, like the Troglodytes [s]; others that pronounce without opening their lips [t]; and the Phaſians, a Greek people, had, as has been ſaid of the Engliſh [u], a hoarſe voice: an unkind climate forms harſh ſounds, and conſequently the organs of ſpeech cannot be very delicate.

The ſuperiority of the Greek tongue is inconteſtible: I do not ſpeak now of its richneſs, but only of its harmony. For all the northern tongues, being over-loaded with conſonants [w], are too often apt to offend with an unpleaſing auſterity; whereas the Greek

[s] Plin. Hiſt. Nat. L. V. c. 8.

[t] Lahontan Memoir. T. II. p. 217. Conf. Wöldike de ling. Grönland, p. 144, & ſeq. Act. Hafn. T. II.

[u] Clarmont de Aere, Locis, & aquis Angliæ. Lond. 1672. 12.

[w] Wotton's Reflex. upon ancient and modern Learning, p. 4. Pope's Letter to Mr. Walſh, T. I. 74.

tongue

tongue is continually changing the conſonant for the vowel, and two vowels, meeting with but one conſonant, generally grow
into a diphthong [x]. The ſweetneſs of the
tongue admits of no word ending with theſe
three harſh letters Θ, Φ, X, and for the
ſake of Euphony, readily changes letters
for their kindred ones. Some ſeemingly
harſh words cannot be objected here ; none
of us being acquainted with the true Greek
or Roman pronunciation. All theſe advantages gave to the tongue a flowing ſoftneſs,
brought variety into the ſounds of its words,
and facilitated their inimitable compoſition.
And from theſe alone, not to mention the
meaſure which, even in common conver-
ſation, every ſyllable enjoyed, a thing to be
deſpaired of in occidental tongues ; from
theſe alone, I ſay, we may form the higheſt
idea of the organs by which that tongue
was pronounced, and may more than con-

[x] Lakemacher Obſerv. Philolog. P. III. Obſerv.
IV. p. 250, &c.

jecture

jecture, that, by the language of the *Gods*, Homer meant the Greek, by that of *Men*, the Phrygian tongue.

It was chiefly owing to that abundance of vowels, that the Greek tongúe was preferable to all others, for expreſſing by the ſound and diſpoſition of its words the forms and ſubſtances of things. The diſcharge, the rapidity, the diminution of ſtrength in piercing, the ſlowneſs in gliding, and the ſtopping of an arrow, are better expreſſed by the ſound of theſe three verſes of Homer, Iliad Δ.

125. Λίγξε βιὸς, νευρὴ δὲ μέγ᾽ ἴαχεν, ἄλλο δ᾽ ὀϊσὸς ʸ
135. Διὰ μὲν ἄρ᾽ ζωσῆρῶ ἐλήλαῖο δαιδαλέοιο,
136. Καὶ διὰ θωρηκῶ πολυδαιδάλυ ἠρήρεισο,

than even by the words themſelves. You ſee it diſcharged, flying through the air, and piercing the belt of Menelaus.

The deſcription of the Myrmidons in battle-array, Iliad Π. v. 215.

Ἀσπὶς ἄρ᾽ ἀσπίδ᾽ ἔρειδε, κόρυς κόρυν ἀνέρα δ᾽ ἀνήρ.

ʸ Th' impatient weapon whizzes on the wing;
Sounds the tough horn, and twangs the quiv'ring
string, &c. POPE.

2 is

is of the ſame kind, and has never been hit by any imitation : what beauties in one line !

Plato's periods were, from their harmony, compared [y] to a noiſeleſs ſmooth-running ſtream. But we ſhould be miſtaken in confining the tongue to the ſofter harmonies only : it became a roaring torrent, boiſterous as the winds by which Ulyſſes' ſails were torn, ſplit only in three or four places by the words, but rent by the ſound into a thouſand tatters [z]. This was the " *vivida expreſſio*," the living ſound ; ſupremely beautiful, when properly and ſparingly uſed !

How quick, how refined muſt the organs have been, which were the depoſitaries of ſuch a tongue ! The Roman itſelf could not attain its excellence : nay, a Greek father, of the ſecond century of the chriſtian

[y] Longin. Περι υ↓. Sect. 13. §. 1.

[z] Odyſſ. λ. v. 71. Conf. Iliad. ſ. v. 363. & Euſtath. ad h. l. p. 424. L. 10. edit. Rom.

æra,

æra[a], complains of the horrid found of the Roman laws.

Nature keeps proportion; confequently the frame of the Greeks was of a fine clay, of nerves and mufcles moft fenfibly elaftic, and promoting the flexibility of the body: hence that eafinefs, that pliant facility, accompanied with mirth and vigour, which animated all their actions. Imagine bodies moft nicely balanced between leannefs and corpulency: both extremes were ridiculed by the Greeks, and their poets fneer at the Philefiafes[b], Philetafes[c], and Agoracritufes[d].

But though they were beautiful, and by their law early initiated into pleafure, they were not effeminate Sybarites. As an inftance of which we fhall only repeat what Pericles pleaded in favour of the Athenian manners, againft thofe of Sparta, which

[a] Gregor. Thaumat. Orat. Paneg. ad Origen. 49.
[b] Ariftoph. Ran. v. 1485.
[c] Athen. Deipnof. L. XII. c. 13. Ælian. V. H. I. ix. 14.
[d] Ariftoph. Equit.

were

were as different from thoſe of the reſt of
Greece, as their public oeconomy was:
" The Spartans, ſays Pericles, employ their
" youth to get, by violent exerciſes, manly
" ſtrength : but we, though living indo-
" lently, encounter every danger as well as
" they; calmly, not anxiouſly, mindful of
" its approaches, we meet it with voluntary
" magnanimity, and without any compul-
" ſion of the law. Not diſconcerted by its
" impending threats, we meet its moſt fu-
" rious attacks, with no leſs boldneſs than
" they, whom perpetual practice has pre-
" pared for its ſtrokes. We are fond of
" elegance, without loving finery; of ge-
" nius, without being emaſculate. In ſhort,
" to be fit for every great enterprize, is the
" characteriſtic of the Athenians °."

I cannot, nor will I pretend to fix a rule
without allowing exceptions. There was
a Therſites in the army of the Greeks. But
it is worth obſerving, that the beauty of a
nation was always in proportion to their cul-

° Thucyd. L, II. c. 39.

tiva-

tivation of the arts. Thebes, wrapt up in a mifty fky, produced a fturdy uncouth race[f], [g] according to Hippocrates's obfervation on fenny, watry foils[h]; and its fterility in producing men of genius, Pindar only excepted, is an old reproach. Sparta was as defective in this refpect as Thebes, having only Alcman to boaft of; but the reafons were different: whereas Attica enjoyed a pure and ferene fky, which refined the fenfes[i], and of courfe fhaped their bodies in proportion to that refinement; and Athens was the feat of arts. The fame remark may be made with regard to Sicyon, Corinth, Rhodes, Ephefus, &c. all which having been fchools of the arts, could not want convenient models. The paffage of Ariftophanes, infifted on in the letter[k], I

[f] Horat. L. II. Ep. I. v. 244.

[g] Cicero de fato. c. 4.

[h] Περι τοπων. p. 204.

[i] Cicero Orat. c. 8. Conf. Dicæarch. Geogr. edit. H. Steph. c. 2. p. 16.

[k] Nubes, v. 1365.

take

take for a joke, as it really is—and thereby hangs a tale: to have the parts, whereon

> *Sedet æternumque ſedebit*
> *Infelix Theſeus,*   Virg.

moderately complete, were Attick beauties. Theſeus [1], made priſoner by the Theſprotians, was delivered from his captivity by Hercules, but not without ſome loſs of the parts in queſtion; a loſs bequeathed to all his race. This was the true mark of the Theſean pedigree; as a natural mark, repreſenting a ſpear [m], ſignified a Spartan extraction; and we find the Greek artiſts imitating in thoſe places the ſparing hand of nature.

But this liberality of nature was confined to Greece, in a narrower ſenſe. Its colonies underwent the ſame fate, which its eloquence met with when going abroad. " As ſoon, " ſays Cicero [n], as eloquence ſet out from

---

[1] Schol. ad Ariſtoph. Nub. v. 1010.

[m] Plutarch. de Sera Numin. Vindicta, p. 563. 9.

[n] Cicero de Orat.

" the

" the Athenian port, fhe plumed herfelf
" with 'the manners of all the iflands in
" her way, adopted the Afiatick luxury,
" and forfaking her found Attick expref-
" fion, loft her health." The Ionians,
tranfplanted by Nileus from Greece into
Afia, after the return of the Heraclides,
grew ftill more voluptuous beneath that
glowing fky. Heaps of vowels brought
wantonnefs into every word; the neighbour-
ing iflands partook of their climate and
manners, which a fingle Lefbian coin may
convince us of[o]. No wonder then, if their
bodies degenerated as much from thofe of
their anceftors, as their manners.

The remoter the colonies the greater the
difference. Thofe Greeks, who had chofen
their abode in Africa, about *Pithicuffa*, fell
in with the natives in adoring apes; nay,
even gave the names of thofe animals to
their children[p].

[o] Golzius, Tab. XIV. T. II,
[p] Diodorus Sic. L. XX. p. 763. al. 449.

M   The

The modern Greeks, though compofed of various mingled metals, ftill betray the chief mafs. Barbarifm has deftroyed the very elements of fcience, and ignorance over-clouds the whole country; education, courage, manners are funk beneath an iron fway, and even the fhadow of liberty is loft. Time, in its courfe, diffipates the remains of antiqui-ty: pillars of Apollo's temple at Delos [q], are now the ornaments of Englifh gardens: the nature of the country itfelf is changed. In days of yore the plants of Crete [r] were fa-mous over all the world; but now the ftreams and rivers, where you would go in queft of them, are mantled with wild luxu-riant weeds, and trivial vegetables [s].

Unhappy country! How could it avoid being changed into a wildernefs, when fuch

[q] Stukely's Itinerar. III. p. 32.

[r] Theophraft. Hift. Pl. L. IX. c. 16. p. 1131. l. 7. ed. Amft. 1644. fol. Galen de Antidot. I. fol. 63. B. I. 28. Idem de Theriac. ad Pifon. fol. 85. A. I. 20.

[s] Tournefort Voyage, Lett. I. p. 10. edit. Amft.

popu-

populous tracts of land as Samos, once mighty enough to balance the Athenian power at fea, are reduced to hideous defarts ' !

Notwithftanding all thefe devaftations, the forlorn profpect of the foil, the free paffage of the winds, ftopped by the inextricable windings of entangled fhores, and the want of almoft all other commodities ; yet have the modern Greeks preferved many of the prerogatives of their anceftors. The inhabitants of feveral iflands, (the Greek race being chiefly preferved in the iflands), near the Natolian fhore, efpecially the females, are, by the unanimous account of travellers, the moft beautiful of the human race ".

Attica ftill preferves its air of philanthropy ": all the fhepherds and clowns welcomed the two travellers, Spon and Wheeler ; nay, pre-

' Belon. Obferv. L. II. ch. 9. p. 151. a.
ᵘ Idem. L. III. ch. 34. p. 350. b. Corn. le Brun. V. fol. p. 169.
ᵂ Dicæarch. Geogr. c. 1. p. 1.

vented

vented them with their falutations [x] : neither have they loft the Attick falt, or the enterprifing fpirit of the former inhabitants [y].

Objections have been made againft their early exercifes, as rather derogating from, than adding to, the beauteous form of the Greek youths.

Indeed, the continual efforts of the nerves and mufcles feem rather to give an angular gladiatorial turn, than the foft Contour of beauty, to youthful bodies. But this may partly be anfwered by the character of the nation itfelf: their fancy, their actions, were eafy and natural ; their affairs, as Pericles fays, were managed with a certain carelefsnefs, and fome of Plato's dialogues [z] may give us an idea of that mirth and chearfulnefs which prevailed in all the Gymnaftick exercifes of their youth. Hence his defire of having thefe places, in his common-

[x] Voyage de Spon et Wheeler, T. II. p. 75, 76.
[y] Wheeler's Journey into Greece, p. 347.
[z] Conf. Lyfis, p. 499. Edit. Fref. 1602.

wealth,

wealth, frequented by old folks, in 'order
to remind them of the joys of their youth *.

Their games commonly began at ſun
riſe ᵇ; and Socrates frequented them at that
time.   They choſe the morning-hours, in order to avoid being incommoded by the heat :
as ſoon as their garments were laid down,
the body was anointed with the elegant Attick oil, partly to defend it from the bleak
morning-air; as it was uſual to practice,
even during the ſevereſt cold ᶜ; and partly to prevent a too copious perſpiration,
where it was intended only to carry off
ſuperfluous humours ᵈ.   To this oil they
aſcribed alſo a ſtrengthening quality ᵉ.   The

ᵃ De Republ.
ᵇ De Leg. L. VII. p. 892, l. 30—6. Conf. Petiti
Leg. att. p. 296. Maittaire Marm. Arund. p. 483.
Gronov. ad Plaut. Bacchid. v. Ante Solem Exorien-
tem.
ᶜ Galen. de Simpl. Medic. Facult. L. II. c. 5.
fol. 9. A. Opp. Tom. II. Frontin. Stratag. L. I. c. 7.
ᵈ Lucian Gymn. p. 907. Opp. T. II. Edit. Reitz.
ᵉ Dion. Halic. A. R. c. 1. §. 6. de vi dicendi in
Demoſt. c. 29. Edit. Oxon.

exerciſes

exerciſes being over, they went to bathe,
and there ſubmitted to a freſh unction ; and
a perſon leaving the bath in this ſtate " appears, ſays Homer, taller, ſtronger, and
ſimilar to the immortal Gods '·

We may form a very diſtinct idea of the
different kinds and degrees of wreſtling
among the ancients, from a vaſe once in
the poſſeſſion of Charl. Patin, and, as he
gueſſes, the urn of a gladiator ⁸.

Had it been a prevailing cuſtom among
the Greeks to walk, either barefooted, like
the heroes in their performances ʰ, or with
a ſingle ſole, as we commonly believe, their
feet muſt have been bruiſed.   But there are
many inſtances of their extreme nicety in
this reſpect ; for, they had names for above
ten different ſorts of ſhoes ¹.

ᶠ 'OΔ. T. v. 230.

⁸ Numiſm. Imp. p. 160.

ʰ Philoſtrat. Epiſt. 22. p. 922. Conf. Macrob. Sat.
L. V. c. 18. p. 357. Edit. Lond. 1694. 8. Hygin.
Sat. 12.

¹ Conf. Arbuthnot's Tabl. of Anc. Coins, ch. 6.
p. 116.

The

The coverings of the thighs were thrown off at the publick exercifes, even before the flourifhing of the art [k]; which was a great advantage to the artifts. As for the nourifhment of the wreftlers in remoter times, I found it more proper to mention milk in general, than foft cheefe.

If I remember right, you think it ftrange, and even undemonftrable, that the primitive church fhould have dipped their profelytes, promifcuoufly : confult the note [l].

As I am now entering upon the difcuffion of my fecond point, I could wifh that thefe probabilities of a more perfect nature, among the Greeks, might be allowed to have fome conclufive weight; and then I fhould have but a few words to add.

[k] Thucyd. L. I. c. 6. Euftath ad Iliad. ᛊ. p. 1324. l. 16.

[l] Cyrilli Hierof. Catech. Myftag. II. c. 2, 3, 4. p. 284. ed. Thom. Miles, Oxon. 1703. fol. 305. Vice Comitis Obferv. de Antiq. Baptifini rit. L. IV. c. 10. p. 286—89. Binghami Orig. Ecclef. T. IV. L. XI. c. 11. Godeau Hift. de l'Eglife, T. I. L. III. p. 623.

Charmo-

Charmoleos, a Megarian youth, a ſingle kiſs of whom was valued at two talents[m], was, no doubt, beautiful enough to ſerve for a model of *Apollo :* Him, *Alcibiades, Charmides,* and *Adimanthus*[n], the artiſts could ſee and ſtudy to their wiſh for ſeveral hours every day : and can you imagine thoſe trifling opportunities propoſed to the Pariſian artiſts, equivalents for the loſs of advantages like theſe ? But granting that, pray, what is there to be ſeen more in a ſwimmer than in any other perſon ? The extremities of the body you may ſee every where. As for that author[o], who pretends to find in France beauties ſuperior to thoſe of *Alcibiades,* I cannot help doubting his ability to maintain what he aſſerts.

What has been ſaid hitherto might alſo

[m] Lucian. Dial. Mort. X. §. 3.
[n] Idem. Navig. E. 2. p. 248.
[o] De la Chambre Diſcours ; où il eſt prouvé que les François ſont les plus capables de tous les peuples de la perfection de l'eloquence, p. 15.

. an-

2

anfwer the objection drawn from the judgment of our academies, concerning thofe parts of the body which ought to be drawn rather more angular than we find them in the antiques. The Greeks, and their artifts, were happy in the enjoyment of figures endowed with youthful harmony; for, we have no reafon to doubt their exactnefs in copying nature, if we only confider the angular fmartnefs with which they drew the wrift-bones. *Agafias*'s celebrated *Gladiator*, in the *Borg-hefe*, has none of the modern angles, nor the bony prominences authorifed by our ar-tifts : all his angular parts are thofe we meet with in the other Greek ftatues. And this ftatue, which was perhaps one of thofe that were erected, in the very places where the games were held, to the memory of the feveral victors, may be fuppofed an exact copy of nature. The artift was bound to reprefent any victor in the very attitude, and inftantaneous motion, in which he overcame

his

his antagoniſt, and the *Amphictyones* were the judges of his performance[p].

Many authors having written on this, and the following point of the treatiſe, I have contented myſelf with giving a few remarks of my own. Superficial arguments, in matters of this kind, can neither ſuit the deeper views of our times, nor lead to general concluſions. Nevertheleſs we do not want authors whoſe premature deciſions often get the better of their judgment, and that not in matters concerning the art alone. Pray, what deciſions of an author may be depended upon, who, when deſigning to write on the arts in general, ſhews himſelf ſo ignorant of their very elements, as to aſcribe to *Thucydides*, whoſe conciſe and energetick ſtyle was not without difficulties, even for *Tully*[q], the character of ſimplicity?[r] Another of

[p] Lucian. pro Imagin. p. 490. Edit. Reitz. T. II.
[q] Cic. Brut. c. 7. & 83.
[r] Conſiderations ſur les Revolutions des Arts. Paris, 1755. p. 33.

that

that tribe, feems as little acquainted with *Diodorus Siculus,* when he defcribes him as hunting after elegance[*]. Nor want we blockheads enough who admire, in the ancient performances, fuch trifles as are below any reafonable man's attention. " The " rope, fays a travelling fcribler, which ties " together Dirce and the ox, is to connoif- " feurs the moft beautiful object of the " whole groupe of the Toro Farnefe[t]."

Ah mifer ægrota putruit cui mente falillum!

I am no ftranger to thofe merits of the modern artifts which you oppofe to the ancients: but at the fame time I know, that the imitation of thefe alone has elevated the others to that pitch of merit; and it would be eafy to prove that, whenever they for-

---

[*] Pagi Difcours fur l'Hiftoire Grecque, p. 45.
[t] Nouveau Voyage d'Hollande, de l'Allem. de Suiffe & d'Italie, par M. de Blainville.

fook

fook the ancients, they fell into the faults of thofe, whom alone I intended to blame.

Nature undoubtedly mifled Bernini: a *Carita* of his, on the monument of Pope Urban the VIIIth, is faid to be corpulent, and another on that of Alexander the VIIth, even ugly [u]. Certain it is, that no ufe could be made of the Equeftrian ftatue of Lewis XIV. on which he had beftowed fifteen years, and the King immenfe fums. He was reprefented as afcending, on horfeback, the mount of honour: but the action both of the rider and of the horfe was exaggerated, and too violent; which was the caufe of baptizing it a Curtius plunging into the gulph, and its having been placed only in the Thuilleries: from which we may infer, that the moft anxious imitation of nature is as little fufficient for attaining beauty, as the ftudy of anatomy alone for attaining the jufteft proportions: thefe Lairefle, by his own ac-

[u] Richardfon's Account, &c. 294, 295.

count,

count, took from the ſkeletons of Bidloo;
but, though a profeſſor in his art, committed many faults, which the good Roman ſchool, eſpecially Raphael, cannot be
charged with. However, it is not meant
that there is no heavineſs in his Venus; nor
does it clear him from the faults imputed to
him in the Maſſacre of the Innocents, engraved by Marc. Antonio, as has been attempted
in a very rare treatiſe on painting ᵂ; for there
the female figures labour under an exuber-
ance of breaſts; whereas the murderers look
ghaſtly with leanneſs : a contraſt not to be
admired : the ſun itſelf has ſpots.

Let Raphael be imitated in his beſt manner, and when in his prime; thoſe works
want no apology : it was to no purpoſe to
produce Parrhaſius and Zeuxis in order to
excuſe Him, and the Dutch proportions!
'Tis true, the paſſage of Pliny ˣ, which you

ᵂ Chambray Idée de la Peint. p. 46. **au Mans,**
1662. 4to.

ˣ Plin. Hiſt. Nat. L. XXXV. c. 10.

quote

quote concerning Parrhaſius, meets commonly with the ſame interpretation, viz. *that, ſhunning corpulency he fell into leanneſs* [y]. But ſuppoſing Pliny to have underſtood what he wrote, we muſt clear him of contradicting himſelf. A little before he allowed to Parrhaſius a ſuperiority in the contour, or in his own words, *in the outlines*; and in the paſſage before us, *Parrhabaſius, compared with himſelf, ſeems, in* POINT OF THE MIDDLE PARTS, *to fall ſhort of himſelf.* The queſtion is, what he means by middle parts? Perhaps the parts bordering on the outlines: but is not the deſigner obliged to know every poſſible attitude of the frame, every change of its contour? If ſo, it is ridiculous to give this explication to our paſſage: for the middle parts of a full face are the outlines of its profile, and ſo on. Conſequently, there is no ſuch thing

[y] (Durand) Extrait de l'Hiſtoire de la Peint. de Pline. p. 56.

as

as middle parts to be met with by a deſigner : the idea of a painter, well-ſkilled in
the contour of the outlines, but ignorant of
their contents, is an abſurd one. Parrhaſius perhaps either wanted ſkill in the Chiar-
oſcuro, or Keeping in the diſpoſition of his
limbs, and this ſeems the only explication,
which the words of Pliny can reaſonably
admit of. Unleſs we chooſe to make him
another La Fage, who, though a celebrated
deſigner, never failed ſpoiling his contours
with his colours. Or, perhaps, to indulge
another conjecture, Parrhaſius ſmoothed the
outlines of his contour, where it bordered
on the grounds, in order to avoid being
rough ; a fault committed, as it ſeems, by
his contemporaries, and by the artiſts who
flouriſhed in the beginning of the ſixteenth
century, who circumſcribed their figures, as
it were with a knife ; but thoſe ſmooth contours wanted the ſupport of keeping, and of
maſſes gradually riſing or ſinking, in order
to become round, and to ſtrike the eye : by
fail-

failing in which, his figures got an air of flatneſs; and thus Parrhaſius fell ſhort of himſelf, without being either too corpulent or too lean.

We cannot conclude, from the Homeric ſhape which Zeuxis gave his female figures, that he raiſed them, like Rubens, into fleſh-hills. There is ſome reaſon to believe, from the education of the Spartan ladies, that they had ſomething of a maſculine vigour, though they were the chief beauties of Greece; and ſuch a one is the Helena of Theocritus.

All this makes me doubt of finding among the ancients any companion for Jacob Jordans, though he is ſo zealouſly defended in your letter. Nor am I afraid of maintaining what I have ſaid concerning him. Mr. d'Argenville is indeed a very induſtrious collector of criticiſms upon the artiſts; but as his deſign is not very extenſive, ſo his deciſions are often too general, to afford us characteriſtical ideas of his heroes.

A good

A good eye muſt be allowed to be a better judge, in matters of this kind, than all the ambiguous deciſions of authors : and to fix the character of Jordans, I might content myſelf with appealing to his Diogenes, and the Purification, in the royal cabinet at Dreſden. But, for the reader's ſake, let me inquire into the meaning of what you call *Truth* in painting. For if truth, in the general ſenſe, can by no means be excluded from any branch of the arts, we have, in the deciſion of Mr. d'Argenville, a riddle to unfold, which, if it has any meaning at all, muſt have the following :

Rubens, enabled by the inexhauſtible fertility of his genius, to pour forth fictions like Homer himſelf, diſplays his riches even to prodigality : like him he loved the marvellous, as well in thought and grandeur of conception, as in compoſition, and chiar'oſcuro. His figures are compoſed in a manner unknown before him, and his lights, jointly darting upon one great maſs, diffuſe

N   over

over all his works a bold harmony, and amazing fpirit. Jordans, a genius of a lower clafs, cannot, in the ideal part of painting, by any means be compared with his great mafter. He had no wings to foar above nature ; for whieh reafon he humbly followed, and painted her as he found her: and if this be *truth*, he, no doubt, had a larger fhare of it than Rubens.

If the modern artifts, with regard to forms and beauty, are not to be direƈted by antiquity, there is no authority left to in-fluence them. Some, in painting Venus, would give her a Frenchified air [z]; another would prefent her with an Aquiline nofe, the Medicean Venus, as they would fay, having fuch a one [a]: her hands would be provided with fpindles inftead of fingers ;

[z] Obfervat. fur les Arts & fur quelques morceaux de Peint. & de Sculpt. expofés au Louvre, 1748. p. 65.

[a] Nouvelle Divifion de la Terre par les differentes Efpeces d'Hommes, &c. dans le Journ. des Sçav. 1704. Avr. 152.

and

and she would ogle us with Chinese eyes, like the beauties of a new Italian school. Every artist, in short, would, by his performance, betray his country : but, as Democritus says [b], if the artists ought to pray the gods to let them meet with none but auspicious images, those of the ancients will best suit their wishes.

Let us, however, make some exception in favour of Fiamingo's children. For, lustiness and full health being the common burden of the praises of children, whose infant forms are not strictly susceptible of that beauty, which belongs to the steadiness of riper years; the imitation of his children has reasonably become a fashion among our artists. But neither this, nor the indulgence of the academy at Vienna, can be, or indeed was meant to be decisive, in favour of the modern children ; it only leads us to make a distinction. The ancients

---

[b] Plutarch. Vit, Æmil. p. 147. ed. Bryani. T. II.

went

went beyond nature, even in their children : the moderns only follow her; and, provided their infant forms, exuberant as they are, do not influence their ideas of youthful and riper bodies, they may be allowed to be in the right, though, at the fame time, the ancients were not in the wrong.

Our artifts are, likewife, at full liberty to drefs the hair of their figures as they pleafe: but, being fo fond of nature, they muft needs know, that it is nature which fhades, with pendant locks, the forehead and temples of all thofe, whofe life is not fpent between the comb and the looking-glafs: and finding this manner carefully obferved in moft ftatues of the ancients, they may take it as a proof of their attachment to fimplicity and truth ; a proof of the more weight, as they did not want people, bufier in adorning their bodies than their minds, and as nice in adjufting their hair, as the moft elegant of our European courtiers. But it was commonly looked upon as a mark of

an

an ingenuous and noble extraction, to dreſs the hair in the manner of the ſtatues [c].

The imitation of the ancient contour has indeed never been rejected, not even by thoſe whoſe chief want was that of correctneſs: but we differ about imitating that " noble ſimplicity and ſedate grandeur" in their works. An expreſſion which hath ſeldom met with general approbation, and never pronounced without hazard of being miſ-underſtood.

In the Hercules of Bandinelli, the idea of it was deemed a fault [d]: an uſurpation on Raphael's Maſſacre of the Innocents [e].

The idea of " nature at reſt," I own, might, perhaps, produce figures like the young Spartans of Xenophon ; nor would the bulk of mankind be better pleaſed with performances in the taſte of my treatiſe, (ſuppoſing even all its precepts authoriſed

[c] Lucian. Navig. S. Votum. c. 2. p. 249.
[d] Borghini Ripoſo, L. II. p. 129.
[e] Chambray Idée de la Peint. p. 47.

by

by the judges of the art) than with a ſpeech
made before the Areopagites.   But it is not
on the bulk of mankind that we ought to
confer the legiſlative power in the art.
And though works of an extenſive compoſition ought certainly to have the ſupport
of a vigour and ſpirit proportioned to their
extent, yet there are limits which muſt not
be overleapt : uſe not ſo much ſpirit as to
repreſent the everlaſting Father like the cruel
God of war, or an ecſtaſied ſaint like a
prieſteſs of Bacchus.   .

Indeed, in the eyes of one unacquainted
with this characteriſtick of the ſublime, a
Madonna of Treviſani will ſeem preferable
to that of Raphael in the royal cabinet at
Dreſden.   I know that even artiſts were of
opinion, that its being placed ſo near one of
the former, was not a little diſadvantageous
to it.   Hence it ſeemed not ſuperfluous to
enquire into the true grandeur of that in-
eſtimable picture, as it is the only production

duction of this Apollo of painters, that Germany is poſſeſſed of.

No compariſon, indeed, is to be made of its compoſition with that of the tranſ-figuration; which, however, I think fully compenſated by its being genuine : whereas Julio Romano might perhaps claim one half of the other as his own. The difference of the hands is viſible: but in the Madonna, the ſpirit of that epoch, in which Raphael performed his Athenian ſchool, ſhines with ſo full a luſtre, as to make even the autho-rity of Vaſari ſuperfluous.

'Tis no eaſy matter to convince a critick, conceited enough to blame the Jeſus of the Madonna, that he is miſtaken. Pythagoras, ſays an antient philoſopher[f], and Anaxa-goras look at the ſun with different eyes: the former ſees a God, the latter a ſtone. We want but experience to diſcover truth and beauty in the faces of Raphael, with-

---

[f] Maxim. Tyr. Diſſ. 25. p. 303. Edit. Markl.

out

out enquiring into their dignity: beauty pleaſes, but ſerious graces charm[g]. Such are the beauties of the ancients, which gave that ſerious air to Antinous, which we generally aſcribe to his ſhading locks. Sudden raptures, or the enticement of a glance, are often momentary; let an attentive eye dwell upon thoſe confuſed beauties which the tranſient look conveys, and the paint will vaniſh. True charms owe their durability to reflection, and hidden graces allure our enquiries: reluctant and unſatisfied we leave a coy beauty, in continual admiration of ſome new-fancied charm: and ſuch are the beauties of Raphael and the ancients; not agreeably trifling ones, but regular and full of real graces[h]. By that Cleopatra became the beauty of all enſuing ages: nobody[i] was aſtoniſhed at her face, but her air engaged every eye, and ſubdued

[g] Vide Spectator, N. 418.
[h] Philoſtrat. Icon. Anton. p. 91.
[i] Plutarch. Ant

the

the melted heart. A French Venus at her toilet is much like Seneca's wit: which, if put to the teſt, diſappears [k].

The compariſon of Raphael and ſome of the moſt celebrated Dutch, and new Italian painters, concerns only the management, (*Trattamento*). The endeavours of the former of theſe, to hide the laborious induſtry that appears in all their works, gives an additional ſanction to my judgment; for, hiding is labour. The moſt difficult part in performances of the arts, is to ſpread an air of eaſineſs, the " UT SIBI QUIVIS " over them [l]; of which, among the ancients, the pictures of Nicomachus were entirely deſtitute [m].

All this, however, is not meant to derogate from Vanderwerf's ſuperior merit: his works give a luſtre even to the cabinets of kings. He diffuſed over them an inconceiv-

---

[k] Obſervat. ſur les Arts, &c, p. 65.
[l] Quintil. L. IX. c. 14.
[m] Plutarch. Timoleon. P, 142.

able

able polifh; every trace of his pencil, one would think, is molten; and, in the colliquation of his tints, there reigns but one predominant colour. He might be faid to have enamelled rather than painted.

His works indeed pleafe. But does the character of painting confift in pleafing alone? Denner's bald pates pleafe likewife. But what, do you imagine, would the wife ancients think of them? Plutarch, from the mouth of fome Ariftides or Zeuxis, would tell him, that beauty never dwells in wrinkles [n].

'Tis faid, the Emperor Charles VI. when he firft faw one of Denner's pictures, was loud in its praife, and in admiration of his induftry. The painter was immediately defired to make a fellow to the firft, and was magnificently rewarded: but the Emperor,

---

[n] Plutarch. Adul. & Amici difcrim. p. 53. D.

com-

comparing each of them with some pieces
of Rembrant and Vandyke, declared, "that
having now satisfied his curiosity, he would
on no account have any more from this artift." An English nobleman was of the
fame opinion: for being shewn a picture of
Denner's, "You are in the wrong, said he,
if you believe that our nation esteems performances, which owe their merits to industry rather than to genius."

I am far from applying these remarks to
Vanderwerf; the difference between him
and Denner is too great: I only joined them
in order to prove, that a picture which
only pleafes can no more pretend to univerfal approbation than a poem. No; their
charms muft be durable; but here we meet
with caufes of difguft in the very parts,
where the painter endeavoured to pleafe
us.

Thofe parts of nature that are beyond
obfervation, were the chief objects of thefe

2   painters:

painters : they were particularly cautious of changing the fituation even of the minuteft hair, in order to furprize the moft fharp-fighted eye with all the microcofm of nature.   They may be compared to thofe difciples of Anaxagoras, who placed all human wifdom in the palm of the hand—but mark, as foon as they attempt to ftretch their art beyond thefe limits, to draw larger proportions, or the nudities, the painter appears

Infelix operis fummâ, quia ponere totum
        nefcit.

                                        Hor.

Defign is as certainly the painter's firft, fecond, and third requifite, as action is that of the orator.

I readily allow the folidity of your remarks, concerning the " reliefs" of the ancients.   In my treatife I myfelf charged them with a want of fufficient fkill in per-
                                ·fpective ;

ſpective; and hence the faults in their reliefs.

The fourth point chiefly concerns *Alle-*
gory.

In painting we commonly call fiction allegory : for, though imitation ariſes from
the very principles of painting as well as of
poetry, it conſtitutes, by itſelf, neither of
them °. A picture, without allegory, is but
a vulgar image, and reſembles Davenant's
Gondibert, an epopée without fiction.

Colouring and deſign are to painting
what metre and truth, or the fable, are to
poetry; a body without ſoul. Poetry, ſays
Ariſtotle, was firſt inſpired with its ſoul,
with fiction, by Homer; and with that the
painter muſt animate his work. Deſign and
colouring are the fruits of attention and
practice : perſpective and compoſition, in
the ſtricteſt ſenſe, are eſtabliſhed or fixed
rules; they are of courſe but mechanical;

° Ariſtot. Rhet. L. I. c. 11. p. 61. Edit. Lond.
1619. 4to. Plato Phæd. p. 46. I. 44.

and, if I may be allowed the expreſſion, only mechanical ſouls are wanting to underſtand and to admire them.

Pleaſures in general, ſave only thoſe which rob the bulk of mankind of their invaluable treaſure, time, become durable, and are free from tedioufneſs and difguſt, in proportion as they engage our intellectual faculties. Mere ſenſual ſentiments ſoon languiſh ; they do not influence our reaſon : ſuch is the delight we take in the common landſcape, flower, and fruit paintings : the artiſt, in performing them, thinks but very little; and the connoiſſeur, in conſidering them, thinks no more.

A mere hiſtory-piece differs from a landſcape only in the object : in the former you draw facts and perſons, in the latter, ſky, land, ſeas, &c. both, of courſe, being founded on the ſame principle, imitation, are eſſentially but of one kind.

If it be not a contradiction to ſtretch the limits of painting, as far as thoſe of poetry,

and

and confequently, to allow the painter
the fame ability of elevating himfelf to the
pitch of the poet as the mufician enjoys;
it is clear that hiftory, though the fublimeft
branch of painting, cannot raife itfelf to the
heighths of tragick or epick poetry, by imitation alone.

Homer, as Cicero tells us[p], has tranf-
formed man into God: which is to fay; he
not only exceeded truth, but, to raife his
fiction, preferred even the impoffible, if
probable, to the barely poffible[q]. In this
Ariftotle fixes the very effence of poetry, and
tells us that the pictures of Zeuxis had that
characteriftick. The poffibility and truth,
which Longinus requires of the painter, as
oppofites to abfurdity in poetry, are not con-
tradictory to this rule.

This heighth the hiftory-painter cannot
reach, only by a contour above common nature, or a noble expreffion of the paffions:

[p] Cicero Tufc. L. I. c. 28.
[q] Ariftot. Poet. c. 28.

for

for thefe are requifite in a good portrait-
painter, who is able to execute them without diminifhing the likenefs of his model.
They are but imitation, only prudently
managed. The heads of Vandyke are
charged with too exact an obfervation of nature; an exactnefs that would be faulty in
a hiftory-piece.

Truth, lovely as it is in itfelf, charms
more, penetrates deeper, when invefted with
fiction: fable, in its ftricteft fenfe, is the
delight of childhood; allegory that of riper
years. And the old opinion, that poetry was
of earlier date than profe, as unanimoufly
attefted by the annals of different people,
makes it evident, that even in the moft bar-
barous times, truth was preferred, when appearing in this drefs.

Our underftanding, moreover, labours under the fault of beftowing its attention chiefly
on things, whofe beauties are not to be perceived at firft fight, and of inadvertently
flighting others, becaufe clear as day: images
of

of this kind, like a fhip on the waves, leave but momentary traces in our memory. Hence the ideas of our childhood are the moft per-manent, becaufe every common occurrence then feems extraordinary. Thus, if nature herfelf inftructs us, that fhe is not to be moved by common things, let art, as the Orator, ad Herennium, advifes us, follow her dictates.

Every idea increafes in ftrength, if ac-companied by another or more ideas, as in comparifons; and the more ftill as they differ in kind: for ideas, too analogous to each other, do not ftrike: as for inftance, a white fkin compared to fnow. Hence the power of difcovering a fimilarity, in the moft different things, is what we commonly call wit; Ariftotle, " unexpected ideas: and thefe he requires in an orator '. The more you are furprized by a picture, the more you are affected; and both thofe ef-

---

' Ariftot. Rhet. III. c. 2. §. 4.

O   fects

fects are to be obtained by allegory, like to fruit hid beneath leaves and branches, which when found ſurprizes the more agreeably, the leſs it was thought of. The ſmalleſt com-poſition is ſuſceptible of the ſublimeſt powers of art: all depends upon the idea.

Neceſſity firſt taught the artiſts to uſe allegory. No doubt, they began with the repreſentation of ſingle objects of one claſs: but as they improved, they attempted to ex-preſs what was common to many particu-lars; *i. e.* general ideas. All the qualities of ſingle objects afford ſuch ideas: but to become general, and at the ſame time ſen-ſible, they cannot preſerve the particular ſhape of ſuch or ſuch an object, but muſt be ſubmitted to another ſhape, eſſential to that object, but a general one.

The Egyptians were the firſt, who went in ſearch of images of that kind. Such were their hieroglyphicks. All the deities of antiquity, eſpecially thoſe of Greece, nay, their very names, were originally Egyp-

tian.

tian'. Their perfonal theology was quite allegorical; and fo is ours. But the fymbols of thefe inventors, partly preferved by the Greeks, were often fo myfterioufly arbitrary, as to make it altogether impoffible to find out their meaning, even by the help of thofe authors that are ftill extant; and fuch a dif-covery was looked upon as a nefarious pro-fanation'. Thus facredly myfterious was the pomegranate " in the hand of the Samian Juno: and to divulge the Eleufinian rites, was thought worfe than the robbery of a temple ".

The relation of the fign to the thing fig-nified, was in fome meafure founded on the known or pretended qualities of the latter. The Egyptian Horfemarten was of that kind; an image of the fun, becaufe his fpecies was

---

* Herodot. L. II. c. 50.

t Herodot. L. II. c. 3. c. 47. Conf. L. II. c. 61· Paufan. L. II. p. 71. l. 45. p. 114. l. 57. L. V. p. 317. l. 6.

u Paufan. L. II. c. 17. p. 149. l. 24.

w Arrian. Epict. L. III. c. 21. p. 439. Edit. Up-ton.

faid

ſaid to have no female, and to live ſix months under and ſix above ground [x]. In like manner the cat, being ſuppoſed to bring forth a number of kittens equal to that of the days in a month, became the ſymbol of Iſis, or the moon [y],

The Greeks, on the contrary, endowed with more wit, and undoubtedly with more ſenſibility, made uſe of no ſigns but ſuch as had a true relation to the thing ſignified, or were moſt agreeable to the ſenſes: all their deities they inveſted with human forms [z]. Wings, among the Egyptians, were the ſymbol of eager and effectual ſervices; a ſymbol conformable to their nature, and continued by the Greeks: and if the Attick *Victoria* had none, it was meant to ſignify, that ſhe had choſen Athens for her

[x] Plutarch. de Iſid. & Oſir. p. 355. Clem. Alex. Strom. L. V. p. 657, 58. Edit. Potteri. Ælian. Hiſt. Anim. L. 10. c. 15.

[y] Plut. L. C. p. 376. Androvand. de Quadr. digit. Vivipar. L. III. p. 574.

[z] Strabo, L. XVI. p. 760. al. 1104.

abode.

abode [a]. A goofe, among the Egyptians, was the fymbol of a cautious leader; in confequence of which the prows of their fhips were formed like geefe [b]. This the Greeks preferved alfo, and the ancient *Roftrum* refembled the neck of a goofe [c].

Of all the figures, whofe relation to their intended meaning is fomewhat obfcure, the Sphinx perhaps alone was continued by the Greeks. Placed in the front of a temple, it was, among the Greeks, almoft as inftructive, as it was fignificant among the Egyptians [d]. The Greek Sphinx was winged [e], its head bare, without that ftole which it wears on fome Attick coins [f].

---

[a] Paufan. L. III. p. 245. l. 21.

[b] Kircher Oedip. Æg. T. III. p. 64. Lucian. Nav. 3 Vol. c. 1. Bayf. de re Nav. p. 130. edit. Baf. 1537. 4.

[c] Schaffer de re Nav. L. III. c. 3. p. 196. Pafferii Luc. T. II. tab. 93.

[d] Lactant. adv. 253. L. VII. Thebaid.

[e] Beger. Thef. Palat. p. 234. Numifm. Mufell. Reg. et Pop. T. 8.

[f] Haym. Teforo Britt. T. I. p. 168.

O 3   It

It was in general a characteriſtic of the Greeks, to mark their productions with a certain chearfulneſs : the muſes love not hideous phantoms : ánd Homer himſelf, when by the mouth of ſome god he cites an Egyptian allegory, always cautiouſly begins with " WE ARE TOLD." Nay, the elder Pampho [g], though he exceeds the Egyptian oddities, by his deſcription of Jupiter wrapt up in horſe-dung, approaches nevertheleſs the ſublime idea of the Engliſh poet :

As full, as perfect, in a hair as heart ;
As full, as perfect, in vile man that mourns,
As the rapt ſeraph, that adores and burns.

                                        Pope.

It will be no eaſy matter to find, among the old Greek coins, an image like that of a ſnake encircling an egg [h], on a Syrian coin of the third century. None of their monu-

[g] Ap. Philoſtr. Heroic. p. 693.
[h] Vaillant Num. Colon. Rom. T. II. p. 136. Conf. Bianchini Iſtor. Unic. p. 74.

                                        ments

ments are marked with any thing ghaſtly :
of theſe they were, if poſſible, ſtill more
cautious than of ill-omen'd words. The
image of death is not to be ſeen, perhaps,
but on one gem [i], and that in the ſhape commonly exhibited at their feaſts [k]; *viz.* dancing to a flute, with intent to make them
enjoy the preſent pleaſures of life, by re-
minding them of its ſhortneſs. On another
gem [l], with a Roman inſcription, there is a
ſkeleton, with two butterflies as images of
the ſoul, one of which is caught by a bird;
a pretended ſymbol of the metempſychoſis :
but the performance is of latter times.

It has been likewiſe obſerved, that [m] among
thoſe myriads of altars, ſacred even to the
moſt whimſical deities, there never was one
ſet apart to death; ſave only on the ſolitary

[i] Muſ. Flor. T. I. Tab. 91. p. 175.

[k] Petron. Sat. c. 34.

[l] Spon. Miſcell. Sect. I. Tab. 5.

[m] Kircher Oedip. T. III. p. 555. Cuper de Elephant. Exercit. c. 3. p. 32.

coaſts,

coaſts, which were deemed the borders of the world [n].

The Romans, in their beſt times, thought like the Greeks; and always, in adopting the iconology of a foreign nation, traced the footſteps of theſe their maſters. An elephant, one of the latter myſterious ſymbols of the Egyptians [o] (for there is on the moſt ancient monuments neither elephant [p] nor hart, oſtrich nor cock, to be found), was the image of different things [q], and perhaps of eternity, as on ſome Roman [r] coins, becauſe of his longevity. But on a coin of the emperor Antoninus, this animal, with the inſcription, MUNIFICENTIA, cannot poſſibly hint at any other thing but the grand games, the magnificence of which was augmented by thoſe animals.

[n] In Extremis Gadibus. v. Euſtath. ad Il. A. p. 744. l. 4. ad. Rom. Id. ad Dionyſ. Περιηγ. ad v. 453. p. 84. Ed. Oxon. 1712.

[o] Kircher Oed. Aeg. T. III. p. 555.

[p] Horapoll. Hierogl. L. II. c. 84.

[q] Cuper. l. c. Spanh. Diſſ. T. I. p. 169.

[r] Agoſt. Dialog. II. p. 68.

But

But it is no more my deſign to attempt an inquiry into the origin of every allegorical ſymbol among the Greeks and Romans, than to write a ſyſtem of allegory. All I propoſe is, to defend what I have advanced concerning it, and at the ſame time to direct the artiſt to the images of thoſe ancients, in preference to the iconologies and ill-judged ſymbols of ſome moderns.

We may, from a little ſpecimen, form a judgment of the turn of mind of thoſe ancients, and of the poſſibility of ſubjecting abſtracted ideas to the ſenſes. The ſymbols of many a gem, coin, and monument, enjoy their fixed and univerſally received interpretation; but ſome of the moſt memorable, not yet brought to a proper ſtandard, deſerve a nearer determination.

Perhaps the allegory of the ancients might be divided, like painting and poetry in general, into two claſſes, *viz.* the *ſublime,* and the *more vulgar.* Symbols of the one might be thoſe by which ſome mythological

or

or philofophical allufion, or even fome unknown or myfterious rite, is expreffed.

Such as are more commonly underftood,
viz. perfonified virtues, vices, &c. might be
referred to the other.

The images of the former give to performances of the art the true epick grandeur :
one fingle figure is fufficient to give it : the
more it contains, the fublimer it is : the
more it engages our attention, the deeper it
penetrates, and we of courfe feel it the
more.

The ancients, in order to reprefent a child
dying in his bloom, painted him carried off
by Aurora[s]: a ftriking image ! taken, perhaps, from the cuftom of burying youths at
day-break. The ideas of the bulk of our
artifts, in this refpect, are too trivial to be
mentioned here.

The animation of the body, one of the
moft abftracted ideas, was reprefented by

----

[s] Homer. OΔ. E. v. 121. Conf. Heraclid. Pontic.
de Allegoria Homeri. p. 492. Meurf. de funere. c. 7.

the

the lovelieft, moft poetical images. An artift, who fhould imagine he could exprefs this idea by the Mofaick creation, would be miftaken; for his image would be merely hiftorical, and nothing but the creation of Adam: a hiftory altogether too facred for being either admitted as the allegory of a mere philofophical idea, or into every place: neither does it feem poetical enough for the flights of the art. This idea appears on coins and gems [t], as defcribed by the moft ancient poets and philofophers: Prometheus forming a man of that clay, of which large petrified heaps were found in Phocis in the time of Paufanias [u]; and Minerva holding a butterfly, as an image of the foul, over his head. The fnake encircling a tree behind Minerva, on the above coin of Antoninus Pius, is a fuppofed fymbol of his prudence and fagacity.

[t] Venuti Num. max. moduli. T. 25. Rom. 1739. fol. Bellori Admir. fol. 30.
[u] Paufan. L. X. p. 806. l. 16.

It

It cannot be denied that the meaning of many an ancient allegory is merely conjectu- ral, and therefore not to be applied on every occaſion. A child catching a butterfly on an altar was pretended to ſignify *Amicitia ad aras*, or, " which is not to exceed the bor- ders of juſtice [w]." On another gem, Love, endeavouring to pull off the branch of an old tree, where a nightingale is perching, is ſaid to allegorize love of wiſdom [x]. *Eros, Himeros*, and *Pathos*, the ſymbols of Love, Appetite, and Deſire, are repreſented, they ſay [y], on a gem, encompaſſing the ſacred fire on an altar; Love behind the fire, his head only over-reaching the flames; Appetite and Deſire on both ſides of the altar; Appetite with one hand only in the fire, with the other holding a gar- land; Deſire with both his hands in the flames. A *Victoria* crowning an anchor, on a coin of king Seleucus, was formerly re-

[w] Licet. Gem. Anul. c. 48.
[x] Beger. Theo. Brand. T. 1. p. 182.
[y] Ibid. p. 281.

garded

garded as an image of peace and fecurity pro-
cured by victory, till by the help of hiftory
we have been enabled to give it its true interpretation. Seleucus is faid to have been
born with a mark refembling an anchor [z],
which not only he himfelf, but all his de-
fcendants, the Seleucidæ, have preferved on
their coins [a].

There is another Victoria with butterfly's
wings [b], faftened on a trophy. This, they
fay, is the fymbol of a hero, who, like
Epaminondas, died in the very act of conquering. At Athens fuch a ftatue [c], and an
altar to an unwinged Victoria, was the
fymbol of their perpetual fuccefs in battle:
ours may admit of the fame explication as
Mars in chains at Sparta [d]. Nor was fhe, as
I prefume, provided at random with wings
ufually given to Pfyche, her own being

[z] Juftin. L. XV. c. 4. p. 412. edit. Gronov.
[a] Spanh. Diff. T. I. p. 407.
[b] Ap. D. C. de Moezinsky.
[c] Pauf. L. V. p. 447. l. 22.
[d] Ibid. L. 1. p. 52. l. 4.

thofe of an eagle: they perhaps fignify the foul of the deceafed: however, all thefe conjectures might be tolerable, if a Victoria faftened on trophies of conquered enemies could reafonably correfpond with their being vanquifhed.

Indeed the fublimer allegory of the ancients has not been tranfmitted to us, without the lofs of its moft valuable treafures: it is poor, when compared with the fecond kind, which is often provided with feveral fymbols for one idea. Two different ones, fignifying the happinefs of the times, are expreffed on coins of the emperor Commodus: the one a lady*, fitting with an apple or ball in her right, and a dial in her left hand, beneath a leafy tree: three children are before her, two in a vafe or flower-pot, the ufual fymbol of fertility: the other reprefents four children, who, as is clear by the things they bear, are the feafons. Both have the fubfcription FELICITAS TEMPORVM.

* Paufan. L. III. p. 245. l. 20. Morel Specim. Rei. N. XII.

But

But theſe, and all the ſymbols that want inſcriptions, are of a lower rank; and ſome of them might as well be taken for ſigns of different ideas. Hope[f] and Fertility[g], for inſtance, might be Ceres, Nobility[h], Minerva. Patience[i], on a coin of Aurelian, wants her true characteriſtick, as does Erato; and the Parcæ[k] are only by their garments diſtinguiſhed from the Graces. On the contrary, ideas which are often confounded in morality, as Juſtice and Equity, are extremely well diſtinguiſhed by the ancients. The former is repreſented, as drawn by *Gellius*[l], with a ſtern look, a diadem, and dreſſed hair[m]; the latter with a mild countenance, and waving ringlets; ears of corn ariſing from her balance, as ſymbols of the advan-

---

[f] Spanhem. Diſſ. T. I. p. 154.
[g] Spanhem. Obſ. ad Juliani Imp. Orat. I. p. 282.
[h] Montfaucon Ant. expl. T. III.
[i] Morell. Specim. Rei Num. T. VIII. p. 92.
[k] Artemidor. Oneirocr. L. II. c. 49.
[l] Noct. Attic. L. XIV. c. 4.
[m] Agoſt. Dialog. II. p. 45. Rom. 1650. fol.

tages

tages of equity; and ſometimes ſhe holds in her other hand [n] a cornu-copia.

Peace, on a coin of the emperor Titus, is to be ranked among thoſe of a more ener-getick expreſſion. The goddeſs of Peace leans on a pillar with her left arm, in the hand of which ſhe holds the branch of an olive-tree, whilſt the other waves the ca-duceus over the thigh of a victim on a little altar, which hints at the bloodleſs ſacrifices of that goddeſs: the victims were ſlaughtered out of the temple, and nothing but the thighs were offered at the altar, which was not to be ſtained with blood.

Peace uſually appears with the olive-branch and the caduceus, as on another coin of this emperor [o]; or on a ſtool placed on a heap of arms, as on a coin of Druſus [p]. On ſome of Tiberius's and Veſpaſian's coins [q] Peace appears in the act of burning arms.

[n] Triſtan. Comm. hiſt. de l'Emp. T. I. p. 297.
[o] Numiſm. Muſell. Imp. R. tab. 38.
[p] Ibid. Tab. II.
[q] Ibid. Tab. XXIX. Eriſſo Dichiaraz. di Medagl. ant. P. II. p. 130.

2

On

On a coin of the Emperor Philip there is a noble image; a fleeping Victory: which, with better reafon, may be taken for the fymbol of confidence in conqueft, than for that in the fecurity of the world; as the in fcription pretends. Of an analogous idea was the picture, by which the Athenian General Timotheus was ridiculed, for the blind luck with which he obtained his victories: he was reprefented afleep, with Fortune catching Towns in her Net [r].

The Nile, with his fixteen children, is of this fame clafs [s]. The child that reaches the ears of corn, and the fruits, in his Cornu, is the fymbol of the higheft fertility; but thofe that over-reach them are figns of mifcarrying feafons. Pliny explains the whole [t]. Egypt is at the height of its fertility, when the Nile rifes fixteen feet: but if it either falls fhort of, or exceeds that

[r] Plutarch Syll. p. 50, 51.
[s] Conf. Philoftrat. Imag. p. 737.
[t] Plin. Hift. N. L. XVIII. c. 47. Agoft. Dial. III. p. 104.

meafure

meaſure, it equally blaſts the land with un-
fruitfulneſs. Roſſi, in his collection, neglected the children.

Satyrical pictures belong alſo to this claſs:
the Aſs of Gabrias, for inſtance [u], which
imagines itſelf worſhipped by the people,
as they bow to the ſtatue of Iſis on its
back. It is impoſſible to give a live-
lier image of the pride of the Vulgar-
Great.

The ſublimer allegory might be ſupplied
by the lower claſs, had it not met with the
ſame fate. We are, for inſtance, not acquainted with the figure of Eloquence, or
Peitho; or that of the Goddeſs of Comfort,
Parergon, repreſented by Praxiteles, as Pauſanias tells us [w]. Oblivion had an altar a-
mong the Romans [x], and perhaps a figure:
as may alſo be ſuppoſed of Chaſtity, whoſe

---

[u] Gabriæ Fab. p. 169. in Æſop. Fab. Venet.
1709. 8.

[w] Pauſan. L. I. c. 43. p. 105. L. 7.

[x] Plutarch. Sympoſ. L. IX. qu. 6.

altar

altar is to be found on coins [y]; and of
Fear, to which Thefeus offered facrifices [z].

However, the remains of ancient allegory
are not yet worn out: there are ftill many
fecret ftores: the poets, and other monuments of antiquity, afford numbers of beautiful images. Thofe, who in our time, and
that of our fathers, were bufy in improving
allegory, and in facilitating the endeavours
of the artifts; thofe, I fay, fhould reafonably have had recourfe to fo rich and pure
a fountain. But there was an epoch to appear, in which a fhocking croud of pedants
fhould, with downright madnefs, confpire
in an univerfal uproar againft every the
leaft glimpfe of good tafte. Nature, in their
eyes, was puerile, and ought to be fafhioned:
blockheads, both young and old, vied in
painting devices and emblems, for the benefit
of artifts, philofophers, and divines; and
woe to him who made a compliment, with-

[y] Vaillant Numifm. Imp. T. II. p. 133.
[z] Plutarch. Vit. Thef. p. 26.

out

out dreſſing it up in an emblem ! Symbols void of ſenſe were illuſtrated with in-ſcriptions, giving an account of what they meant, and meant not: theſe are the trea-ſures which are dug for, even in our times, and which, being then in high faſhion, out-ſhone all antiquity had left.

The ancients, for inſtance, repreſented Munificence by a woman holding a Cornu-copia in one hand, and the table of the Ro-man Congiarium in the other [a]: an image which looked too parſimonious for modern liberality; another therefore was contrived [b], with two horns; one of them inverted, the better to pour out its contents; an eagle, the meaning of which is too hard for me to gueſs at, was ſet upon her head; others painted her with a pot in each hand [c]. Eternity was, by the ancients, drawn either

---

[a] Agoſt. Dial. II. p. 66, 67. Numiſm. Muſell. Imp. Rom. Tab. 115.

[b] Ripa Iconol. n. 87.

[c] Theſaur. de Arguta Diƈt.

fitting

ſitting on a Globe, or rather Sphere [d], with a Haſta in her hand; or ſtanding [e], with the Sphere in one hand, and the Haſta in the other; or with the Sphere in her hand, and no Haſta; or elſe covered with a floating Veil [f]. Theſe are the images of Eternity on the coins of the Empreſs Fauſtina: but there was not gravity enough in them for the modern artiſts. Eternity, ſo frightful to many, required a frightful image [g]; a form female down to the breaſt, with Globes in each hand; the reſt of the Body a circling ſtar-marked Snake turning into itſelf.

Providence very often has a Globe at her feet, and a Haſta in her left hand [h]. On a coin of the Emperor Pertinax [i], ſhe ſtretches out both her hands, towards a Globe falling

[d] Numiſm. Muſell. Imp. R. Tab. 107.

[e] Ibid. Tab. 106.

[f] Ibid. Tab. 105.

[g] Ripa Iconol. P. I. n. 53.

[h] Agoſt. Dial. II. p. 57. Numiſm. Muſell. l. c. Tab. 68.

[i] Agoſt. l. c.

from

from the clouds. A female figure, with two heads, feemed more expreffive to the moderns [k].

Conftancy, on fome of Claudius's coins [l], is either fitting or ftanding, with a Helmet on her head, and a Hafta in her left hand; or without Helmet and Hafta, but always with a finger pointing to her face, as if clofely debating fome point. For diftinction fake the moderns joined a couple of pillars [m].

It is very probable, that Ripa was often at a lofs with his own figures. Chaftity, in his Iconology, holds in one hand a Whip [n], (a ftrange incitement to virtue) in the other a Sieve: The firft inventor, perhaps, hinted at Tuccia the veftal; which Ripa not remembring, indulges the moft abfurd whims, not worth repeating.

---

[k] Ripa Ic. P. I. n. 135.
[l] Agoft. Dial. II. p. 47.
[m] Ripa Iconol. P. I. n. 31.
[n] Ibid. P. I. n. 25.

By

By thus contraſting ancient and modern allegory, I mean not to diveſt our times of their right of ſettling new allegories: but from the different manners of thinking, I ſhall draw ſome rules, for thoſe that are to tread theſe paths.

The character of noble ſimplicity was the chief aim of the Greeks and Romans: of which Romeyn de Hooghe has given the very contraſt. His book, in general, may very fitly be compared to the elm in Virgil's hell:

> *Hanc ſedem ſomnia vulgo*
> *Vana tenere ferunt, foliiſque ſub omnibus*
> *hærent.* Æn. VI.

The diſtinctneſs of the ancient allegory was owing to the individuation of its images. Their rule, (if we except only a few of thoſe above-mentioned), was to avoid every ambiguity; a rule ſlightly obſerved by the moderns: the Hart, for inſtance, ſymbolizing [°]

[°] Vide Picinelli Mund. Symb.

baptiſm,

baptifm, revenge, remorfe, and flattery; the Cedar, a preacher, worldly vanities, a fcholar, and a woman dying in the pangs of child-birth.

That fimplicity and diftinctnefs were always accompanied by a certain decency. A hog fignifying, among the Egyptians, a fcrutator of myfteries [p], together with all the fwine of Cæfar Ripa and fome of the moderns, would have been thought, by the Greeks, too indecent a fymbol of any thing whatever: fave only where that animal made part of the arms of a place, as it appears to be on the Eleufinian coins [q].

The laft rule of the ancients was to beware of figns too near a-kin to the thing fignified. Let the young allegorift obferve thefe rules, and ftudy them, jointly with mythology, and the remoteft hiftory.

Indeed fome modern allegories, (if thofe ought to be called modern that are entirely

[p] Shaw Voyag. T. I.
[q] Hayman Teforo Brit. T. I. p. 219.

in

in the tafte of antiquity), may perhaps be compared with the fublimer clafs of the ancient.

Two brothers of the Barbarigo-family, immediately fucceeding each other [r], in the dignity of Doge of Venice, are allegorized by Caftor and Pollux [s]; one of whom, as the fable tells us, gave the other part of that immortality which Jupiter had conferred on him alone. Pollux, in the allegory, prefents his brother, reprefented by a fkull, with a circling fnake, as the fymbol of eternity; on the reverfe of a fictitious coin, beneath the defcribed figures, there drops a broken branch from a tree, with the Virgilian infcription,

Primo avulfo non deficit alter.

Another idea on one of Lewis XIVth's

---

[r] Egnatius de exempl. illuftr. Vir. Venet. L. V. p. 133.

[s] Numifm. Barbar. Gent. n. 37. Padova. 1732. fol.

coins,

coins, is as worthy of notice; being ſtruck[t] on occaſion of the Duke of Lorrain's quit-ing his dominions, after the ſurrender of Marſal, for having betrayed both the French and Auſtrian courts. The Duke is Proteus overcome by the arts of Menelaus, and bound, after having, in vain, tried all his different forms. At a diſtance the con-quered citadel is to be ſeen, and the year of its ſurrender marked in the inſcription. There was no occaſion for the ſuperfluous epigraph : *Protei Artes deluſæ.*

Patience, or rather a longing earneſt de-ſire[u], repreſented by a female figure, with folded hands, gazing on a watch, is a very good image of the lower claſs. It muſt in-deed be owned, that the inventors of the moſt pictureſque allegories have contented themſelves with the remains of antiquity ; none having been authoriſed to eſtabliſh

---

[t] Medailles de Louis le Grand, a. 1663. Paris 1702. fol.

[u] Theſaur. de Argut. Dict.

images

images of their own fancy, for the general imitation of the artiſts. Neither has any attempt of latter times deſerved the honour : for in the whole Iconology of Ripa, of two or three that are tolerable ones,

Nantes in gurgite vaſto ;

an Ethiopian waſhing himſelf, as an alluſion to labour loſt [w], is perhaps the beſt. There are indeed images, and uſeful hints, diſperſed in ſome books of greater note, (as for in-ſtance, The Temple of Stupidity in the Spec-tator [x],) which ought to be collected, and made more general. Thus, were the trea-ſures of ſcience joined to thoſe of art, the time might come, when a painter would be able to repreſent an ode, as well as a tra-gedy.

I ſhall myſelf ſubmit to the publick ſome images : for rules inſtruct, but examples ſtill more. Friendſhip, I find every where

---

[w] Ripa Iconol. P. II. p. 166.
[x] Spectator, Edit. 1724. Vol. II. p. 201.

pitifully

pitifully repreſented, and its emblems are not worth mentioning: their flying ſcribbled labels ſhew us the depth of their inventors.

This nobleſt of human virtues I would paint in the figures of thoſe two immortal friends of heroic times, Theſeus and Pirithous. The head of the former is ſaid to be on gems [y]: he likewiſe appears with the club [z] won from Periphetes, a ſon of Vulcan, on a gem of Philemon. Theſeus conſequently might be drawn with ſome reſemblance. Friendſhip, at the brink of danger, might be taken from the idea of an old picture at Delphos, as deſcribed by Pauſanias [a]. Theſeus was painted in the action of defending himſelf and his friend againſt the Theſprotians, with his own ſword in one hand, and another drawn from the ſide of his friend, in the other. The beginning of their friendſhip, as deſcribed by Plu-

[y] Canini Imag. des Heros. N. I.
[z] Stoch Pier. Grav. Pl. LI.
[a] Pauſan. L. X. p. 870. 871.

tarch,

tarch [b], might also be an image of that idea. I am astonished not to have met, among the emblems of the great men of the Barbarigo-family, with an image of a good man and eternal friend. Such was Nicolas Barbarigo, who contracted with Marco Trivisano a friendship worthy of immortality ;

Monumentum ære perennius :

a little rare treatise alone has preserved their memory [c].

A little hint of Plutarch's might furnish an image of Ambition: he mentions [d] the sacrifices of Honour, as being performed bareheaded ; whereas all other sacrifices, save only those of Saturn [e], were offered with covered heads. This custom he believes to

[b] Vit. Thesei. p. 29.

[c] De Monstrosa Amicitia respectu perfectionis inter Nic. Barbar. & Marc. Trivisan. Venet. apud Franc. Baba. 1628. 4.

[d] Vita Marcelli. Ortelii Capita Deor. L. II. fig. 41.

[e] Thomasin. Donar. Vet. c. 5.

have

3

have taken its riſe from the uſual ſalutation in ſociety; though it may as well be *vice verſa:* perhaps it ſprung from the Pelaſgian rites [f], which were performed bareheaded. Honour is likewiſe repreſented by a female figure, crowned with laurels, a *Cornucopia* and *Haſta* in her hands [g]. Accompanied by Virtue, a male figure with a helmet, ſhe is to be found on a coin of Vitellius [h]: and the heads of both on thoſe of Gordian and Galien [i].

Prayers might be perſonified from an idea of Homer. Phœnix, the tutor of Achilles, endeavouring to reconcile him to the Greeks, makes uſe of an allegory. " Know Achil-
" les, ſays he, that prayers are the daughters
" of Zeus [k]; they are bent with kneeling;
" their faces ſorrowful and wrinkled, with

[f] Plutarch. Quæſt. Rom. P. 266. F.
[g] Vulp. Latium. T. I. L. I. c. 27. p. 406.
[h] Agoſtin. Dialog. II. p. 81.
[i] Ibid. & Beger Obſ. in Num. p. 56.
[k] Iliad. i. v. 498. Conf. Heraclides Pontic. de Allegoria Homeri, p. 457, 58.

3   " eyes

" eyes lifted up to heaven. They follow
" Ate ; who, with a bold and haughty
" mien marches on, and, light of foot as
" ſhe is, runs over all the world, to ſeize
" and torment mankind ; for ever endea-
" vouring to eſcape the Prayers, who inceſ-
" ſantly preſs upon her footſteps, in order
" to heal thoſe whom ſhe hath hurt. Who-
" ever honours theſe daughters of Zeus, on
" their approach, may obtain much good
" from them ; but meeting with repulſe,
" they pray their ſire to puniſh by Ate the
" hard-hearted wretch."

The following well-known old fable might
alſo furniſh a new image. Salmacis, and
the youth beloved by her, were changed to
a fountain, unmanning to ſuch a degree,
that

> *Quiſquis in hos fontes vir venerit, exeat inde
> Semivir : & tactis ſubito molleſcat in
> undis,*
>
> Ovid. Metam. L. IV.

The

The fountain was near Halicarnaſſus in Ca-
ria.   Vitruvius[1] thought he had diſcovered
the truth of that fiction : ſome inhabitants
of Argos and Trœzene, ſays he, going thither
with a mind to ſettle, diſpoſſeſſed the Carians and Leleges ; who, ſheltering themſelves among the mountains, began to ha-
raſs the Greeks with their excurſions : but
one of the inhabitants having diſcovered
ſome particular qualities in that fountain,
erected a building near it, for the convenience of thoſe who had a mind to make
uſe of its water.   Greeks and Barbarians
mingled there ; and theſe at length, ac-
cuſtomed to the Greek civility, loſt their
ſavageneſs, and were inſenſibly moulded
into another nature.   The fable itſelf is
well known to the artiſts : but the narrative
of Vitruvius might inſtruct them how to
draw the allegory of a people taught humanity and civiliſed, like the Ruſſians by Pe-

[1] Architect. L. II. c. 8.

ter

ter the Firſt. The fable of Orpheus might ſerve the ſame purpoſe. Expreſſion only muſt decide the choice.

Suppoſing the above general obſervations upon allegory inſufficient to evince its neceſſity in painting, the examples will at leaſt demonſtrate, that painting reaches beyond the ſenſes.

. The two chief performances in allegorical painting, mentioned in my treatiſe, viz. the Luxemburg gallery, and the cupola of the Imperial Library at Vienna, may ſhew how poetical, how happy an uſe their authors made of allegory.

Rubens propoſing to paint Henry IV. as a humane victor, with lenity and goodneſs prevailing, even in the puniſhment of unnatural rebels, and treacherous banditti, repreſents him as Jupiter ordering the gods to overthrow and puniſh the vices: Apollo and Minerva let fly their darts upon them, and the vices, hideous monſters, in a tumultuous uproar tumble over each other:

Q Mars,

Mars, entering in a fury, threatens total deſtruction; but Venus, image of celeſtial Jove, gently lays hold of his arm:—you fancy you hear her blandiſhing petition to the *mailed* god: " rage not with cruel revenge againſt the vices—they are puniſhed."

The whole performance of Daniel Gran [m] is an allegory, relative to the Imperial Library, and all its figures are as the branches of one ſingle tree. 'Tis a painted Epopee, not beginning from the eggs of Leda; but, as Homer chiefly rehearſes the anger of Achilles, this immortalizes only the Emperor's care of the ſciences. The preparations for the building of the library are repreſented in the following manner:

Imperial majeſty appears as a lady ſitting, her head ſumptuouſly dreſſed, and on her breaſt a golden heart, as a ſymbol of the Emperor's generoſity. With her ſceptre ſhe

[m] Vide Repreſentatio Bibliothecæ Cefareæ Viennæ 1737. fol. obt.

gives

gives the ſummons to the builders; at her feet ſits a genius with an angle, palette, and chiſſel; another hovers over her with the figures of the Graces, as ſymbols of that good taſte which prevailed in the whole. Next to the chief figure ſits general Liberality, with a purſe in her hand; below her a genius, with the table of the Roman Congiarius, and behind her the Auſtrian Liberality, her mantle embroidered with larks. Several Genii gather the treaſures that flow from the Cornucopia, in order to diſtribute them among the votaries of the arts and ſciences, chiefly thoſe, whoſe good offices to the library had entitled them to regard. The execution of the Imperi:l orders perſonified, directs her face to the commanding figure, and three children preſent the model of the houſe. Next her an old man, the image of Experience, meaſures on a table the plan of the building, a genius ſtanding beneath him with a plummet, as ready to begin. Next the old man ſits

Inven-

Invention, with a ſtatue of Iſis in her right, and a book in her left hand, ſignifying, that Nature and Science are the fathers of Invention, the puzzling ſchemes of which are repreſented by a Sphinx lying before her.

This performance was compared to the great platfond of Le Moine at Verſailles, with an eye to the neweſt productions of France and Germany alone : for the great gallery of the ſame palace, painted by Charles le Brun, is, without doubt, the ſublimeſt performance of poetick painting, ſince the time of Rubens; and being poſſeſſed of this, as well as of the gallery of Luxemburg, France may boaſt of the two moſt learned allegorical performances.

The gallery of Le Brun contains the hiſtory of Louis XIV. from the Pyrenæan peace, to that of Nimeguen, in nine large, and eighteen ſmaller pieces : that in which the King determines war againſt Holland, contains, in itſelf alone, an ingenious and ſublime application of almoſt the whole

mytho-

mythology °: its beauties are too exuberant
for this treatife; let the artift's ideas be
judged only by two of the fmaller compofitions.   He reprefents the famous paffage
over the Rhine : his hero fits in a chariot,
a thunderbolt in his hand, and Hercules,
the image of heroifm, drives him through
the midft of tempeftuous waves.   The figure
reprefenting Spain is born down by the cur-
rent : the river god, aghaft, lets fall his
oar : the victories, approaching on rapid
wings, prefent fhields, marked with the
names of the towns conquered after the
paffage.   Europa aftonifhed beholds the
fcene.

Another reprefents the conclufion of the
peace.   Holland, though with-held by the
Imperial Eagle, fnatching her robe, runs to
meet peace, defcending from heaven, fur-
rounded by the Genii of gaiety and pleafure,
fcattering flowers all around her.   Vanity,

° This piece is engraved by Simmoneau Senior
Conf. Lepicié Vies des p. P. de R. T. I. p. 64.

crowned

crowned with peacocks feathers, endeavours to with-hold Spain and Germany from following their affociate: but perceiving the cavern where arms are forged for France and Holland, and hearing fame threatening in the fkies, they likewife follow her example. Is not the former of thefe two performances comparable, in fublimity, to the Neptune of Homer, and the ftrides of his immortal horfes?

But let examples be never fo ftriking, allegory will ftill have adverfaries: they rofe in times of old, againft that of Homer himfelf. There are people of too delicate a confcience, to bear truth and fiction in one piece: they are fcandalized at a poor river-god in fome facred ftory. Pouffin met with their reproaches, for perfonifying the Nile in his Mofes[p]. A ftill ftronger

---

[p] Another reprefentation of that ftory, and one of Pouffin's beft originals, is in the gallery of Drefden, in which the river god is extremely advantageous to the compofition of the whole.

party

party has declared againſt the obſcurity of
allegory; for which they cenſured, and ſtill
continue to cenſure, Le Brun. But who is
there ſo little experienced as not to know,
that perſpicuity and obſcurity depend often
upon time and circumſtances? When Phi-
dias firſt added a tortoiſe ^q to his Venus, 'tis
likely that few were acquainted with his
deſign in it, and bold was the artiſt who
firſt dared to fetter her: time, however,
made the meaning as clear as the figures
themſelves. Allegory, as Plato ſays ^r of
poetry in general, has ſomething enigmatick
in itſelf, and is not calculated for the bulk
of mankind. And ſhould the painter, from
the fear of being obſcure, adapt his performance to the capacity of thoſe, who look
upon a picture as upon a tumultuous mob,
he might as well check every new and extraordinary idea. The deſign of the famous
Fred. Barocci, in his Martyrdom of St. Vi-

^q Plin.
^r Plato Alcibiad. II. P. 457. l. 30.

taliş,

talis, by drawing a little girl alluring a magpye with a cherry, muſt have been very myſterious to many; the cherry * alluding to the ſeaſon, in which that ſaint ſuffered.

The painting of the greater machines, and of the larger parts of publick buildings, palaces, &c. ought to be allegorical. Grandeur is relative to grandeur; and heroick actions are not to be ſung in elegiack ſtrains. But is every fiction allegorical in every place? The Venetian Doge might as well pretend to enjoy his ſuperiority in *Terra firma*. I am miſtaken if the Farneſian gallery is to be ranked among the allegorical performances. Neverthelefs Annibal, perhaps not having it in his power to chooſe his ſubject, may have been too roughly uſed in my treatiſe: it is known that the Duke of Orleans

---

* Baldinucci, Notiz. de 'P. d. D. P. 118. Argenville ſeems not to have underſtood the word, *Ciliegia*: he ſaw that it ſhould be a ſymbol of ſpring, and changed the cherry to a butterfly; the chief object of the picture he omits, and talks only of the girl.

deſired

defired Coypel to paint in his gallery the
hiftory of Æneas[i].

The Neptune of Rubens[u], in the gallery
at Drefden, painted on purpofe to adorn the
magnificent entry of the Infant Ferdinand
of Spain into Antwerp, as governor of the
Netherlands; was there, on a triumphal
arch, allegorical[w]. The god of the ocean
frowning his waves into peace, was a poetick image of the Prince's efcaping the
ftorm, and arriving fafe at Genoa. But
now he is nothing more than the Neptune
of Virgil.

Vafari, when pretending to find allegory
in the Athenian fchool of Raphael[x], *viz.*
a comparifon of philofophy and aftronomy
with theology, feems to have required, and,
by the common opinion of his time, to
have been authorifed to require fomething

---

[i] Lepicie Vies des P. R. P. II. p. 17, 18.
[u] Recueil d'Eftamp. de la Gall. de Drefd. fol. 48.
[w] Pompa & Introitus Ferdinandi Hifp. Inf. p. 15.
Antv. 1641. fol.
[x] Vafari vite. P. III. Vol. I. p. 76.

grand

grand and above the vulgar, in the decorations of a grand apartment : though indeed
there be nothing but what is obvious at firſt
look, and that is, a reprefentation of the
Athenian academy [y].

But in ancient times, there was no ſtory
in a temple, that was not, at the ſame time,
allegorical ; allegory being cloſely interwo-
ven with mythology : the gods of Homer,
ſays an ancient, are the moſt lively images
of the different powers of the univerſe ; ſha-
dows of elevated ideas : and the gallantries of
Jupiter and Juno, in the platfond of a temple of that goddeſs at Samos, were looked
on as ſuch ; air being reprefented by Jupiter,
and earth by Juno [z].

Here I think it incumbent upon me to
clear up what I have ſaid concerning the
contradictions in the character of the Athenians, as reprefented by Parrhaſius. This

[y] Chambray Idée de la P. p. 107, 108. Bellori
Deſcriz. delle Imagini dip. da Raffaello, &c.

[z] Heraclid. Pontic. de Allegoria Homeri, p. 443.

you

you think an eafy matter; the painter having done it either in the hiftorical way, or
in feveral pictures: which latter is abfurd.
Has not there been even a ftatue of that
people, done by Leochares, as well as a
temple[a]? The compofition of the picture
in queftion, has ftill eluded all probable conjectures[b]; and the help of allegory having
been called in, has produced nothing but
Teforo's [c] ghaftly phantoms. This fatal
picture of Parrhafius, I am afraid, will of
itfelf be a perpetual inftance of the fuperior
fkill of the ancients in allegory.

What has been faid already of allegory,
in general, contains likewife what remarks
may be made upon its being applied to decorations; neverthelefs as you infift upon
that point particularly, I fhall lightly mention it too.

There are two chief laws in decoration,

[a] Jofephi Antiq. L. XIV. c. 8. Edit. Haverc.
[b] Dati vite de 'Pittori. p. 73.
[c] Thefaur. Idea Arg. Dict. C. III. p. 84.

viz.

viz. to adorn fuitably to the nature of things and places, and with truth; and not to follow an arbitrary fancy.

The firft, as it concerns the artifts in general, and dictates to them the adjufting of things in fuch a manner, as to make them relative to each other, claims efpecially a ftrict propriety in decorations:

—— *Non ut placidis coeant immitia——*

. Hor.

The facred fhall not be mixed with the profane, nor the terrible with the fublime: this was the reafon for rejecting the fheepsheads [d], in the Doric Metopes, at the chapel of the palace of Luxemburg at Paris.

The fecond law excludes licentioufnefs; nay circumfcribes the architect and decorator within much narrower limits than the painter; who fometimes muft, in fpite of reafon, fubject his own fancy, and Greece, to

[d] Blondel Maifons de Plaifance, T. II. p. 26.

4

fafhion,

fafhion, even in hiftory-pieces: but publick buildings, and fuch works as are made
for futurity, claim decorations that will out-
laft the whims of fafhion; like thofe that,
by their dignity and fuperior excellence, bore
down the attacks of many a century: otherwife they fade away, grow infipid and out
of fafhion, perhaps before the finifhing of
the very work to which they are added.

The former law directs the artift to allegory: the latter to the imitation of antiquity; and this concerns chiefly the fmaller
decorations.

Such I call thofe that make not up of
themfelves a whole, or thofe that are additional to the larger ones. The ancients never applied fhells, when not required by the
fable; as in the cafe of Venus and the Tri-
tons; or by the place, as in the temples of
Neptune: and lamps decked with fhells [c]
are fuppofed to have made part of the imple-
ments of thofe temples. For the fame rea-

[c] Pafferii Lucernæ fict. Tab. 51.

fon

fon they may give luftre, and be very fignificant, in proper places; as in the feftoons
of the Stadthoufe at Amfterdam [f].

Sheep and ox-heads ftripped of their fkin,
fo far from juftifying a promifcuous ufe of
fhells, as the author feems inclined to think,
are plain arguments to the contrary: for they
not only were relative to the ancient facrifices, but were thought to be endowed with
a power of averting lightning [s]; and Numa
pretended to have been fecretly inftructed
about them by Jupiter [h]. Nor can the Corinthian capital ferve for an inftance of a
feemingly abfurd ornament, authorifed and
rendered fafhionable by time alone: for it
feems of an origin more natural and reafon-

[f] Quellinus Maifon de la Ville d'Amft. 1655. fol.

[s] Arnob, adv. Gentes L. V. p. 157. Edit. Lugd.
1651. 4.

[h] An ox-head on the reverfe of an Attick gold
coin, ftamped with the head of Hercules and his club,
is fuppofed to allude to his labours, (Haym. Teforo
Britt. l. 182.) and to be, in general, a fymbol of
ftrength, induftry, or patience, (Hypnerotomachia
Polyphili. Venet. Ald. fol.)

able

able than Vitruvius makes it; which is, however, an enquiry more adapted to a treatife on architecture. Pocock believed that the Corinthian order had not much reputation in the time of Pericles, who built a temple to Minerva: but he fhould have been reminded, that the Doric order belonged to the temples of that goddefs, as Vitruvius informs us [i].

Thefe decorations ought to be treated like architecture in general, which owes its grandeur to fimplicity, to a fyftem of few parts, which being not complex themfelves, branch out into grace and fplendour. Remember here the channelled pillars of the temple of Jupiter, at Agrigentum, (Girgenti now) which were large enough to contain, in one fingle gutter, a man at full length [k]. In the fame manner thefe decorations muft not only be few, but thofe muft likewife confift of few

[i] Vitruv. L. I. c. 2.
[k] Diodor. Sic. L. XIII. p. 375. al. 507.

parts,

parts, which are to appear with an air of grandeur and eaſe.

The firſt law (to return to allegory) might be lengthened out into many a ſub-altern rule : but the nature of things and circumſtances is, and ever muſt be, the ar-tiſt's firſt aim ; as for examples, refutation promiſes rather more inſtruction than authority.

Arion riding on his dolphin, as unmeaningly repreſented upon a Sopra-porta, in a new treatiſe on architecture [1], though a ſignificant image in the apartments of a French Dauphin, would be a very poor one in any place where Philanthropy, or the protection of artiſts like him, could not immediately be hinted at. On the contrary, he would even to this day, though without his lyre, be an ornament to any publick building at Tarentum, becauſe the ancient Tarentines, ſtamped on their eoins the image of Taras,

[d] Blondel Maiſons de Plaiſance.

one

one of the fons of Neptune, riding on a dolphin, on a fuppofition of his being their firft founder.

The allegorical decorations of a building, raifed by the contributions of a whole nation, I mean the Duke of Marlborough's palace at Blenheim, are abfurd: enormous lions of maffy ftone, above two portals, tearing to pieces a little cock [m]. The hint fprung from a poor pun.

Nor can it be denied that antiquity furnifhes fome ideas feemingly analogous to this: as for inftance, the lionefs on the tomb of Leæna, the miftrefs of Ariftogiton, raifed in honour of her conftancy amidft the torments applied by the tyrant, in order to extort from her a confeffion of the confpirators againft him. But from this, I am afraid, nothing can arife in behalf of the above pitiful decoration: that miftrefs of the martyr of liberty having been a notorious woman, and whofe name could

---

[m] Vide Spectator, N°. 51.

R   not

not decently ftand a publick trial. Of the
fame nature are the lizards and frogs on a
temple[n], alluding to the names of the two
architects, Saurus and Batrachus[o]: the a-
bove-mentioned lionefs having no tongue,
made the allegory ftill more expreffive. The
lionefs on the tomb of the famous Lais[p],
holding with her fore-paws a ram, as a
fymbol of her manners[q], was perhaps an
imitation of the former. The lion was, in
general, fet upon the tombs of the brave.

It is not indeed to be pretended that every
ornament and image of the ancient vafes,
tools, &c. fhould be allegorical; and to explain many of them, in that way, would be
equally difficult and conjectural. I am not
bold enough to maintain, that an earthen
lamp[r], in the fhape of an ox's-head, means a
perpetual remembrance of ufeful labours, on

[n] Paufan. L. I. c. 43. l. 22.
[o] Plin. Hift. N. L. XXXVI. c. 5.
[p] Pauf. L. II. c. 2. P. 115. l. 11.
[q] Idem. L. IX. c. 40. P. 795. l. 11.
[r] Aldrovand. de Quadrup. bifulc. p. 141.

account

account of the perpetuity of the fire; nor to decypher here a myfterious facrifice to Pluto and Proferpine'. But the image of a Trojan Prince, carried off by Jupiter, to be his favourite, was of great and honourable fignification in the mantle of a Trojan. Birds pecking grapes feem as fuitable to an urn, as the young Bacchus brought by Mercury to be nurfed by Leucothea, on a large marble vafe of the Athenian Salpion'. The grapes may be a fymbol of the pleafures the deceafed enjoy in Elyfium: the pleafures of hereafter being commonly fuppofed to be fuch, as the deceafed chiefly delighted in when alive. A bird, I need not fay, was the image of the foul. A Sphinx, on a cup facred to Bacchus, is fuppofed to be an allufion to the adventures of Oedipus at Thebes, Bacchus's birth place "; as a

---

* Bellori Lucern. Sepulcr. P. I. fig. 17.
' Spon. Mifc. Sect. II. Art. I. P. 25.
" Vide Buonarotti Offerv. fopra alcuni Medagli. Proem. p. XXVI. Roma. 1693. 4.

Li-

Lizard on a cup of Mentor, may hint at the poffeffor, whofe name perhaps was Saurus.

There is fome reafon to fearch for alle-gory, in moft of the ancient performances, when we confider, that they even built al-legorically. Such an allufive building was a gallery at Olympia [w], facred to the feven liberal arts, and re-echoing feven times a poem read aloud there. A temple of Mer-cury, fupported, inftead of pillars, by Herms, or, as we now fpell, Terms, on a coin of Aurelian [x], is of the fame kind: there is on its front a dog, a cock, and a tongue; figures that want no explication.

Yet the temple of Virtue and Honour, built by Marcellus, was ftill more learnedly executed: having confecrated his Sicilian fpoils to that purpofe, he was difappointed by the priefts, whom he firft confulted on

[w] Plutarch. de Garrulit. p. 502.
[x] Triftan Comment. Hift. des Emper. T. I, p. 632.

that

that defign ; who told him, that no fingle temple could admit of two divinities. Marcellus therefore ordered two temples to be built, adjoining to each other, in fuch a manner that whoever would be admitted to that of Honour muft pafs through that of Virtue [y]; thus publickly indicating, that virtue alone leads to true honour: this temple was near the Porta Capena [z]. And here I cannot help remembering thofe hollow ftatues of ugly fatyrs [a], which, when opened, were found replete with little figures of the graces, to teach, that no judgment is to be formed from outward appearances, and that a fair mind makes amends for a homely body.

Perhaps, Sir, fome of your objections may have been omitted: if fo, it was againft my will——and at this inftant, I remember one

---

[y] Plutarch. Marcell. p. 277.
[z] Vulpii Latium, T. II. L. II. c. 20. p. 175.
[a] Banier Mythol. T. II. L. I. ch. 11. p. 181.

con-

concerning the Greek art of changing blue
eyes to black ones. Diofcorides is the only
writer that mentions it[b]. Attempts of this
kind have been made in our days: a certain Silefian countefs was the favourite beauty
of the age, and univerfally acknowledged
to be perfect, had it not been for her blue
eyes, which fome of her admirers wifhed
were black. The lady, informed of the
wifhes of her adorers, by repeated endeavours overcame nature; her eyes became
black,—and fhe blind.

I am not fatisfied with myfelf, nor perhaps have given you fatisfaction: but the
art is inexhauftible, and all cannot be written. I only wanted to amufe myfelf agreeably at my leifure hours; and the converfa-
tion of my friend FREDERIC OESER, a true
imitator of Ariftides, the painter of the foul,
was not a little favourable to my purpofe:
the name of which worthy friend and ar-

[b] Diofcorid. de Re Med. L. V. c. 179.

tift

tiſt ᶜ ſhall ſpread a luſtre over the end of
my treatiſe.

ᶜ Fred. Oeſer, one of the moſt extenſive geniuſes
which the preſent age can boaſt of, is a German,
and now lives at Dreſden; where, to the honour
of his country, and the emolument of the art, he
gets his livelihood by teaching young blockheads,
of the Saxon-race, the elements of drawing; and by
etching after the Flemiſh painters. N. of Tranſl.

R 4   I N.

INSTRUCTIONS

FOR THE

CONNOISSEUR.

INSTRUCTIONS

FOR THE

CONNOISSEUR.

—————— *Non, ſi quid turbida* ROMA
Elevet, accedas : examenve improbum in illa
Caſtiges trutina : nec te quæſiveris extra.
Nam Romæ eſt Quis non ?——————

YOU call yourſelf a *Connoiſſeur*, and the
firſt thing you gaze at, in conſidering
works of art, is the workmanſhip, the delicacy of the pencilling, or the poliſh given
by the chiſſel.——It was the idea however, its grandeur or meanneſs, its dignity, fitneſs, or unfitneſs, that ought firſt
to have been examined: for induſtry and
talents are independent of each other. A
piece of painting or ſculpture cannot, merely on account of its having been laboured,

4 claim

claim more merit than a book of the ſame ſort. To work curiouſly, and with unneceſſary refinements, is as little the mark of a great artiſt, as to write learnedly is that of a great author.   An image anxiouſly finiſhed, in every minute trifle, may be fitly compared to a treatiſe crammed with quotations of books, that perhaps were never read. Remember this, and you will not be amazed at the laurel leaves of *Bernini*'s Apollo and Daphne, nor at the net held by *Adams*'s ſtatue of water at Potzdam : you will only be convinced that workmanſhip is not the ſtandard which diſtinguiſhes the antique from the modern.

Be attentive to diſcover whether an artiſt had ideas of his own, or only copied thoſe of others ; whether he knew the chief aim of all art, Beauty, or blundered through the dirt of vulgar forms ; whether he performed like a man, or played only like a child.

Books

Books may be written, and works of art executed, at a very ſmall expence of ideas. A painter may mechanically paint a Madonna, and pleaſe; and a profeſſor, in the ſame manner, may write Metaphyſics to the admiration of a thouſand ſtudents. But would you know whether an artiſt deſerves his name, let him invent, let him do the ſame thing repeatedly: for as one feature may modify a mien, ſo, by changing the attitude of one limb, the artiſt may give a new hint towards a characteriſtic diſtinction of two figures, in other reſpects exactly the ſame, and prove himſelf a man. Plato, in *Raphael*'s Athenian ſchool, but ſlightly moves his finger: yet he means enough, and infinitely more than all *Zucchari*'s meteors. For as it requires more ability to ſay much in a few words, than to do the contrary; and as good ſenſe delights rather in things than ſhews, it follows, that one ſingle figure may be the theatre of all an artiſt's ſkill: though, by all that is ſtale and trivial! the bulk of

painters

painters would think it as tyrannical to be fometimes confined to two or three figures, in great only, as the ephemeral writers of this age would grin at the propofal of be-ginning the world with their own private ftock, all public hobby-horfes laid afide: for fine cloaths make the beau. 'Tis hence that moft young artifts,

Enfranchis'd from their tutor's care,

choofe rather to make their entrance with fome perplexed compofition, than with one figure ftrongly fancied and mafterly execut-ed. But let him, who, content to pleafe the few, wants not to earn either bread or applaufe from a gaping mob, let him re-member that the management of a " *little*" more or lefs really diftinguifhes artift from artift; that the truly fenfible produces a multiplicity, as well as quicknefs and delicacy of feelings, whilft the dafhing quack tickles only feeble fenfes and callous organs; that he may confequently be great in fingle
figures,

figures, in the finalleft compofitions, and new and various in repeating things the moft trite. Here I fpeak out of the mouth of the ancients: this their works teach: and both our writers and painters would come nearer them, did not the one bufy themfelves with their words only, the other with their proportions.

In the face of Apollo pride exerts itfelf chiefly in the chin and nether lip; anger in the noftrils; and contempt in the opening mouth; the graces inhabit the reft of his divine head, and unruffled beauty, like the fun, ftreams athwart the paffions. In Laocoon you fee bodily pains, and indignation at undeferved fufferings, twift the nofe, and paternal fympathy dim the eye-balls. Strokes like thefe are, as in Homer, a whole idea in one word; he only finds them who is able to underftand them. Take it for certain, that the ancients aimed at expreffing much in little,

Their

Their ore was rich, and seven times purg'd
   of lead :

whereas moft moderns, like tradefmen in
diftrefs, hang out all their wares at once.
Homer, by raifing all the gods from their
feats, on Apollo's appearing amongft them *,
gives a fublimer idea than all the learning of
Callimachus could furnifh. If ever a prejudice may be of ufe, 'tis here; hope largely
from the ancient works in approaching them,
nor fear difappointments ; but examine, perufe, with cool fedatenefs and filenced paffions, left your difturbed brain find Xenophon flat and Niobe infipid.

To original ideas, we oppofe copied, not
imitated ones. Copying we call the flavifh
crawling of the hand and eyes, after a certain model : whereas reafonable imitation
juft takes the hint, in order to work by itfelf. *Domenichino,* the painter of Tender-
nefs, imitated the heads of the pretended

* Hymn. in Apoll.

                                    Alex-

Alexander at Florence, and of the Niobe at Rome [b]; but altered them like a mafter. On gems and coins you may find many a figure of *Pouffin's* : his Salomon is the Macedonian Jupiter : but whatever his imitation produced, differs from the firft idea, as the bloffoms of a tranfplanted tree differ from thofe that fprung in its native foil.

Another method of copying is, to compile a Madonna from *Maratta*; a S. Jofeph from *Barocci*; other figures from other mafters, and lump them together in order to make a whole. Many fuch altar-pieces you may find, even at Rome; and fuch a painter was the late celebrated *Mafucci* of that city.——Copying I call, moreover, the following a certain form, without the leaft confcioufnefs of one's being a blockhead. Such was he who, by the command of a certain Prince, painted the nuptials of

[b] Alexander, in his S. John, in *St. Andrea della Valle* at Rome; Niobe, in a picture belonging to the *Teforo di S. Gennaro*, at Naples.

Pfyche,

Pſyche, or, if you will, the Queen of Sheba: —
'twas a pity there was no other Pſyche to be
found, but that dangerous one of *Raphael.*
Moſt of the late great ſtatues of the ſaints,
in St. Peter's at Rome, are of the ſame ſtuff
—the block at 500 Roman crowns from
the quarry.

The ſecond characteriſtic of works of art
is Beauty. The higheſt object of meditation for man is man, and for the artiſt
there is none above his own frame. 'Tis by
moving your ſenſes that he reaches your
ſoul: and hence the analyſis of the bodily
ſyſtem has no leſs difficulties for him, than
that of the human mind for the philoſopher. I do not mean the anatomy of the
muſcles, veſſels, bones, and their different
forms and ſituations ; nor the relative meaſure of the whole to its parts, and *vice
verſa :* for the knife, exerciſe, and patience,
may teach you all theſe. I mean the analyſis of an attribute, eſſential to man, but
fluctuating with his frame, allowed by all,
miſ-

I

misconstrued by many, known by few :—
the analysis of beauty, which no definition
can explain, to him whom heaven hath denied a soul for it. Beauty consists in the
harmony of the various parts of an individual. This is the philosopher's stone,
which all artists must search for, though a
a few only find it: 'tis nonsense to him,
who could not have formed the idea out
of himself. The line which beauty describes
is elliptical, both uniform and various: 'tis not
to be described by a circle, and from every
point changes its direction. All this is easily
said; but to apply it——*there is the rub.*
'Tis not in the power of Algebra to determine
which line, more or less elliptic, forms the
divers parts of the system into beauty—but
the ancients knew it; I attest their works,
from the gods down to their vases. The human form allows of no circle, nor has any
antique vase its profile semicircular.

After this, should any one desire me to
assist him more sensibly in his inquiries

concern-

concerning beauty, by ſetting down ſome rules (a hard taſk), I would take them from the antique models, and in want of theſe, from the moſt beautiful people I could meet with at the place where I lived. But to inſtruǎ, I would do it in the negative way; of which I ſhall give ſome inſtances, confining myſelf however to the face.

The form of real beauty has no abrupt or broken parts. The ancients made this principle the baſis of their youthful profile; which is neither linear nor whimſical, though ſeldom to be met with in nature: the growth, at leaſt, of climates more indulgent than ours. It conſiſts in the ſoft coaleſcence of the brow with the noſe. This uniting line ſo indiſpenſibly accompanies beauty, that a perſon wanting it may appear handſome full-faced; but mean, nay even ugly, when taken in profile. *Bernini*, that deſtroyer of art, deſpiſed this line, when legiſlator of taſte, as not finding it in common nature, his only model; and therein was followed by all his school. From this same principle it neceffarily follows, that neither chin nor cheeks, deepmarked with dimples, can be confiftent with true beauty. Hence the face of the Medicean Venus is to be degraded from the firft rank. Her face, I dare fay, was taken from fome celebrated fair one, contemporary with the artift. Two other Venufes, in the garden behind the Farnefe, are manifeftly portraits.

The form of real beauty has neither the projected parts obtufe, nor the vaulted ones fharp. The eye-bone is magnificently raifed, the chin thoroughly vaulted. Thus the beft ancients drew: though, when tafte declined amongft them, and the arts were trampled on in modern times, thefe parts changed too: then the eye-bone became roundifh and obtufely dull, and the chin mincingly pretty. Hence we may fafely affirm, that what they call Antinous, in the

Belve-

Belvedere, whofe eye-bone is rather obtufe, cannot be a work of the higheft antiquity, any more than the Venus.

As thefe remarks are general, they like-wife concern the features of the face, the form only. There is another charm, that gives expreffion and life to forms, which we call Grace; and we fhall give fome loofe reflexions on it feparately, leaving it to others to give us fyftems.

The figure of a man is as fufceptible of beauty as that of a youth: but as a va-rious one, not the various alone, is the Gordian knot, it follows, that a youthful figure, drawn at large, and in the higheft poffible degree of beauty, is, of all pro-blems that can be propofed to the defigner, the moft difficult. Every one may convince himfelf of this: take the moft beautiful face in modern painting, and it will go hard, but you fhall know a ftill more beautiful one in nature.——I fpeak thus, af-

ter

ter having conſidered the treaſures of Rome
and Florence.

If ever an artiſt was endowed with beauty, and deep innate feelings for it; if ever
one was verſed in the taſte and ſpirit of the
ancients, 'twas certainly *Raphael:* yet are
his beauties inferior to the moſt beautiful
nature. I know perſons more beautiful than
his unequalled Madonna, in the *Palazzo
Petti* at Florence, or the Alcibiades in his
academy. The Madonna in the Chriſtmas-
night of *Corregio,* (a piece juſtly celebrated
for its chiar'-oſcuro) is no ſublime idea;
ſtill leſs ſo is that of *Maratta* at Dreſden.
Titian's celebrated Venus [e] in the Tribuna

[e] So are the goddeſſes of the Theopægnia at Blenheim, in Oxfordſhire; and hence it is clear, that
another Venus, analogous to that in the Tribuna,
among the pictures of a gentleman in London, cannot be the production of that genius-in-fleſh only.
This daughter of the Idalian graces ſeems to thrill
with inward pleaſure, and to recollect a night of
bliſs——

There is language in her eye, her cheek, her lip:
Nay, her foot ſpeaks——
SHAKESPEAR.

S 4

at

at Florence is common nature. The little heads of *Albano* have an air of beauty; but it is a different thing to exprefs beauty in little, and in great. To have the theory of navigation, and to guide a fhip through the ocean, are two things. *Pouffin*, who had ftudied antiquity more than his predeceffors, knew perfectly well what his fhoulders could bear, and never ventured into the great.

The Greeks alone feem to have thrown forth beauty, as a potter makes his pot. The heads on all the coins of their Free-ftates have forms above nature, which they owe to the line that forms their profile. Would it not be eafy to hit that line? Yet have all the numifmatic compilers deviated from it. Might not *Raphael*, who complained of the fcarcity of beauty, might not he have recurred to the coins of Syracufe, as the beft ftatues, Laocoon alone excepted, were not yet difcovered?

Far-

Farther than thofe coins no mortal idea *can* go. I wifh my reader an opportunity of feeing the beautiful head of a genius in the Villa Berghefe, and thofe images of un-paralleled beauty, Niobe and her daughters. On the weftern fide of the Alps he muft be contented with gems and paftes. Two of the moft beautiful youthful heads are a Mi-nerva of Afpafius, now at Vienna, and a young Hercules in the Mufeum of the late Baron Stofch, at Florence.

But let no man, who has not formed his tafte upon antiquity, take it into his head to act the connoiffeur of beauty: his ideas muft be a parcel of whims. Of modern beauties I know none that could vie with the Greek female dancer of Mr. *Mengs,* big as life, painted in *Crayons* on wood, for the Marquis Croimare at Paris, or with his Apollo amidft the mufes, in the Villa Al-bano, to whom that of *Guido* in the Aurora, compared, is but a mortal.

All

All the modern copies of ancient gems give us another proof of the deciſive authority of beauty in criticiſms on works of art. *Natter* has dared to copy that head of Minerva mentioned above, in the ſame ſize and ſmaller, but fell ſhort. The noſe is a hair too big, the chin too flat, and the mouth mean. And this is the caſe of modern imitators in general. What can we hope then of ſelf-fancied beauties? Conclude not, however, from this, againſt the poſſibility of a perfect imitation of antique heads: 'tis enough to ſay, that it has not yet exiſted: 'twas probably the fault of the imitators themſelves. *Natter*'s treatiſe on ancient gems is rather ſhallow; and what he wrought and wrote, even on that ſingle branch of engraving, for which he was chiefly celebrated, has neither the ſtrength nor the eaſe of genius.

To this conſciouſneſs of inferiority we owe the ſcarcity of modern ſuppoſititious gems

and

and coins. Any man of tafte may, upon comparifon, diftinguifh even the beft modern coin from the antique original.—I fpeak of the beft antiques: for as to the lower Imperial coins, where the cheat was eafier, the artifts have been liberal enough. *Padoano*'s ftamps, for copying antique coins, are in the Barberini Collection at Rome, and thofe of one *Michel*, a Frenchman, and falfe coiner in tafte, at Florence, in that of the late Baron Stofch.

The third characteriftic of works of art is Execution; or, the fketch being made, the method of finifhing. And even here we commend good fenfe above induftry. As in judging of ftyles, we diftinguifh the good writer by the clearnefs, fluency, and nervoufnefs of his diction; fo in works of art, we difcover the mafter by the manly ftrength, freedom, and fteadinefs of his hand. The auguft contour, and eafinefs of mien, in the figures of Chrift, St. Peter, and the other apoftles, on the right fide of

the

the Transfiguration, speak the classic hand of *Raphael*, as strongly as the smooth, anxious nicety of some of *Julio Romano*'s figures, on the left, the more wavering one of the disciple.

Never admire either the marble's radiant polish, or the picture's glossy surface. For that the journeyman sweated; for this the painter vegetated only. *Bernini*'s Apollo is as polished as HE in the Belvedere; and there is much more labour hid in one of *Trevisani*'s Madonnas, than in that of *Corregio*. Whenever trusty arms and laborious industry prevail, we defy all the ancients. We are not their inferiors even in managing porphyry, though a mob of scriblers, with *Clarencas* in their rear-guard, deny it.

Nor (whatever *Maffei* thinks [d],) did the ancients know a peculiar method of giving a nicer polish to the figures of their concave gems *(Intagli.)* Our artists polish as

[d] Veron. illustr. P. III. c. 7. p. 269.

nicely:

nicely: but ftatues and gems may be de-
teftable, for all their polifh, as a face may be
ugly, with the fofteft fkin.

This however is not meant to blame a
ftatue for its polifh, as it is conducive to
beauty: though Laocoon informs us, that
the ancients knew the fecret of finifhing
ftatues, merely with the chiffel. Nor does
the cleannefs of the pencil, on a picture,
want its merit: yet it ought to be diftinguifhed from enamelled tints. A barked
ftatue, and a briftly picture are alike abfurd.
Sketch with fire, and execute with phlegm.
We blame workmanfhip only as it claims
the firft rank; as in the marbles *à la Bernini*, and the linnen of *Scybold* and *Denner*.

Friend, thefe inftructions may be of ufe.
For as the bulk of mankind amufe themfelves with the fhells of things only, your
eye may be captivated by polifh and glare,
as they are the moft obvious; to put you
on your guard againft which, is leading you
the

the firſt ſtep to true knowledge. For daily obſervation, during ſeveral years, in Italy, has taught me how lamentably moſt young tra- vellers are duped by a ſet of blind leaders. To ſee them ſkip about in the the temple of art and genius, all quite ſober and cool, puts me in mind of a ſwarm of new-fledged graſhoppers wantoning in the ſpring.

O N

ON

GRACE.

ON

G R A C E.

—— Χαριτων ἱμερο φωνων ἱερον φυλον.

GRACE is the harmony of agent and action. It is a general idea: for whatever reaſonably pleaſes in things and actions is gracious. Grace is a gift of heaven ; though not like beauty, which muſt be born with the poſſeſſor : whereas nature gives only the dawn, the capability of this. Education and reflection form it by degrees, and cuſtom may give it the ſanction of nature. As water,

That leaſt of foreign principles partakes,
Is beſt :

So Grace is perfect when moſt ſimple, when freeſt from finery, conſtraint, and affected wit. Yet always to trace nature through the vaſt realms of pleaſure, or through all

T   the

the windings of characters, and circum-
stances infinitely various, seems to require
too pure and candid a taste for this age,
cloyed with pleasure, in its judgments either
partial, local, capricious, or incompetent.
Then let it suffice to say, that Grace can
never live where the passions rave; that
beauty and tranquillity of soul are the centre
of its powers. By this Cleopatra subdued
Cæsar; Anthony slighted Octavia and the
world for this; it breathes through every
line of Xenophon; Thucydides, it seems,
disdained its charms; to Grace Apelles and
Corregio owe immortality; but Michael
Angelo was blind to it; though all the remains of ancient art, even those of but mid-
dling merit, might have satisfied him, that
Grace alone places them above the reach of
modern skill.

The criticisms on Grace in nature, and
on its imitation by art, seem to differ: for
many are not shocked at those faults in the
latter, that certainly would incur their dis-
pleasure

pleasure in the former. This diversity of feelings lies either in imitation itself, which perhaps affects the more the less it is akin to the thing imitated; or in the senses being little exercised, and in the want of attention, and of clear ideas of the objects in question. But let us not from hence infer that Grace is wholly fictitious: the human mind advances by degrees; nor are youth, the prejudices of education, boiling passions, and their train of phantoms, the standard of its real delight—remove some of these, and it admires what it loathed, and spurns what it doted on. Myriads, you say, the bulk of mankind, have not even the least notion of Grace—but what do they know of beauty, taste, generosity, or all the higher luxuries of the soul? These flowers of the human mind were not intended for universal growth, though their seeds lie in every breast.

Grace, in works of art, concerns the human figure only; it modifies the *attitude* and *countenance, dress* and *drapery.* And

T 2   here

here I muſt obſerve, that the following remarks do not extend to the comic part oᶠ
art.

The attitude and geſtures of antique
figures are ſuch as thoſe have, who, con-
ſcious of merit, claim attention as their due,
when appearing among men of ſenſe. Their
motions always ſhew the motive; clear, pure
blood, and ſettled ſpirits; nor does it ſignify whether they ſtand, ſit, or lie; the attitudes of Bacchanals only are violent, and
ought to be ſo.

In quiet ſituations, when one leg alone
ſupports the other which is free, this re-
cedes only as far as nature requires for put-
ting the figure out of its perpendicular. Nay,
in the *Fauni*, the foot has been obſerved to
have an inflected direction, as a token of ſa-
vage, regardleſs nature. To the modern artiſts
a quiet attitude ſeemed inſipid and ſpiritleſs,
and therefore they drag the leg at reſt for-
wards, and, to make the attitude ideal, remove part of the body's weight from the

ſup-

supporting leg, wring the trunk out of its centre, and turn the head, like that of a person suddenly dazzled with lightning. Those to whom this is not clear, may please to recollect some stage-knight, or a conceited young Frenchman. Where room allowed not of such an attitude, they, lest unhappily the leg that has nothing to do might be unemployed, put something elevated under its foot, as if it were like that of a man who could not speak without setting his foot on a stool, or stand without having a stone purposely put under it. The ancients took such care of appearances, that you will hardly find a figure with crossed legs, if not a Bacchus, Paris, or Nireus; and in these they mean to express effeminate indolence.

In the countenances of antique figures, joy bursts not into laughter; 'tis only the representation of inward pleasure. Through the face of a Bacchanal peeps only the dawn of luxury. In sorrow and anguish they re-

T 3　　　　semble

femble the fea, whofe bottom is calm,
whilft the furface raves. Even in the ut-
moft pangs of nature, Niobe continues ftill
the heroine, who difdained yielding to La-
tona. The ancients feem to have taken advantage of that fituation of the foul, in
which, ftruck dumb by an immenfity of
pains, fhe borders upon infenfibility; to exprefs as it were, characters, independent of
particular actions; and to avoid fcenes too
terrifying, too paffionate, fometimes to paint
the dignity of minds fubduing grief.

Thofe of the moderns, that either were
ignorant of antiquity, or neglected to enquire into Grace in nature, have expreffed,
not only what nature feels, but likewife
what fhe feels not. A Venus at Potzdam,
by *Pigal*[1], is reprefented in a fentiment
which

---

[1] " Et toi, rival des Praxiteles & des Phidias ; toi
" dont les anciens auroient employé le cifeau à leur
" faire des dieux capables d'excufer à nos yeux leur
" idolatrie ; inimitable Pigal, ta main fe réfoudra a
" vendre des magots, ou il faudra qu'elle demeure
"   " oifive."

which forces the liquor to flow out at both fides of her mouth, feemingly gafping for breath; for fhe was intended to pant with luft: yet, by all that's defperate! was this very Pigal feveral years entertained at Rome to ftudy the antique. A *Carita* of *Bernini,* on one of the papal monuments in St. Peter's, ought, you'll think, to look upon her children with benevolence and maternal fondnefs; but her face is all a contradiction to this: for the artift, inftead of real graces, applied to her his noftrum, dimples, by which her fondnefs becomes a perfect fneer. As for the expreffion of modern forrow, every one knows it, who has feen cuts, hair torn, garments rent, quite the reverfe of the antique, which, like Hamlet's,

───── *hath that within, which paffeth fhew :*
Thefe, but the trappings, and the fuits of woe.

"oifive." J. J. Rouffeau Difc. fi le Retabl. d. A. S. &c.

This, my dear countryman! is the only paffage of thine, where pofterity will find the orator forgot the philofopher. N. of Tr.

T 4 The

The geftures of the hands of antique figures, and their attitudes in general, are thofe of people that think themfelves alone and un-obferved : and though the hands of but very few ftatues have efcaped deftruction, yet may you, from the direction of the arm, guefs at the eafy and natural motion of the hand. Some moderns, indeed, that have fupplied ftatues with hands or fingers, have too often given them their own favourite attitudes— that of a Venus at her toilet, difplaying to her levee the graces of a hand,

——· *far lovelier when beheld.*

The action of modern hands is commonly like the gefticulation of a young preacher, piping-hot from the college. Holds a figure her cloths? You would think them cob-web. Nemefis, who, on antique gems, lifts her peplum foftly from her bofom, would be thought too griping for any new performance—how can you be fo unpolite to think any thing may be held, without the

the three laſt fingers genteely ſtretched forth ?

Grace, in the accidental parts of antiques, conſiſts, like that of the eſſential ones, in what becomes nature. The drapery of the moſt ancient works is eaſy and ſlight : hence it was natural to give the folds beneath the girdle an almoſt perpendicular direction.— Variety indeed was ſought, in proportion to the increaſe of art ; but drapery ſtill remained a thin floating texture, with folds gathered up, not lumped together, or indiſcreetly ſcattered. That theſe were the chief principles of ancient drapery, you may convince yourſelf from the beautiful Flora in the Campidoglio, a work of Hadrian's times. Bacchanals and dancing figures had, indeed, even if ſtatues, more waving garments, ſuch as played upon the air ; ſuch a one is in the Palazzo Riccardi at Florence ; but even then the artiſts did not neglect appearances, nor exceed the nature of the materials. Gods and heroes are reprefented as the inhabitants of facred places; the dwellings of filent awe, not like a fport for the winds, or as wafting the colours: floating, airy garments are chiefly to be met with on gems—where Atalanta flies

As meditation fwift, fwift as the thoughts
of love.

Grace extends to garments, as fuch were given to the Graces by the ancients.   How would you wifh to fee the Graces dreffed ?   Certainly not in birth-day robes ; but rather like a beauty you loved, ftill warm from the bed, in an eafy negligee.

The moderns, fince the epoch of *Raphael* and his fchool, feem to have forgot that drapery participates of Grace, by their giving the preference to heavy garments, which might not improperly be called the wrappers of ignorance in beauty : for a thick large-folded drapery may fpare the artifts the pains of tracing the Contour under it, as the ancients did.   Some of the modern
figures

figures feem to be made only for lafting. *Bernini* and *Peter* of *Cortona* introduced this drapery. For ourfelves, we choofe light eafy dreffes; why do we grudge our figures the fame advantage?

He that would give a Hiftory of Grace, after the revolution of the arts, would perhaps find himfelf almoft reduced to negatives, efpecially in fculpture.

In fculpture, the imitation of one great man, of *Michael Angelo*, has debauched the artifts from Grace. He, who valued himfelf upon his being " a pure intelligence" defpifed all that could pleafe humanity; his exalted learning difdained to ftoop to tender feelings and lovely grace.

There are poems of his publifhed, and in manufcript, that abound in meditations on fublime beauty: but you look in vain for it in his works.—Beauty, even the beauty of a God, wants Grace, and *Mofes*, without it, from awful as he was, becomes only terrible. Immoderately fond of all that

was

was extraordinary and difficult, he foon broke through the bounds of antiquity, grace, and nature; and as he panted for occafions of difplaying fkill only, he grew extravagant. His lying ftatues, on the ducal tombs of St. Lorenzo at Florence, have attitudes, which life, undiftorted, cannot imitate: fo carelefs was he, provided he might dazzle you with his mazy learning, of that decency, which nature and the place required, that to him we might apply, what a poet fays of St. Lewis in hell:

> *Laiffant le vray pour prendre la grimace,*
> *Il fut toujours au delà de la Grace,*
> *Et bien plus loin que les commandements.*

He was blindly imitated by his difciples, and in them the want of Grace fhocks you ftill more: for as they were far his inferiors in fcience, you have no equivalent at all. How little *Guiliclmo della Porta,*

Porta, the beft of them all, underftood grace and the antique, you may fee in that marble groupe, called the Farnefe-bull; where Dirce is his to the girdle. *John di Bologna, Algardi, Fiammingo,* are great names, but likewife inferior to the ancients, in Grace.

At laft *Lorenzo Bernini* appeared, a man of fpirit and fuperior talents, but whom Grace had never vifited even in dreams. He aimed at encyclopædy in art; painter, architect, ftatuary, he ftruggled, chiefly as fuch, to become original. In his eighteenth year he produced his Apollo and Daphne; a work miraculous for thofe years, and promifing that fculpture by him fhould attain perfection. Soon after he made his David, which fell fhort of Apollo. Proud of general applaufe, and fenfible of his impotency, either to equal or to offufcate the antiques; he feems, encouraged by the daftardly tafte of that age, to have formed the

the project of becoming a legiſlator in art, for all enſuing ages, and he carried his point. From that time the Graces entirely forſook him: how could they abide with a man who begun his career from the end oppoſite to the ancients? His forms he compiled from common nature, and his ideas from the inhabitants of climates unknown to him; for in Italy's happieſt parts nature differs from his figures. He was worſhipped as the genius of art, and univerſally imitated; for, in our days, ſtatues being erected to piety only, none to wiſdom, a ſtatue *à la Bernini* is likelier to make the kitchen proſper than a Laocoon.

From Italy, reader, I leave you to gueſs at other countries. A celebrated *Puget, Girardon,* with all his brethren in *On,* are worſe. Judge of the connoiſſeurs of France by *Watelet,* and of its deſigners, by *Mariette*'s gems.

At

At Athens the Graces ſtood eaſtward, in a ſacred place. Our artiſts ſhould place them over their work-houſes; wear them in their rings; ſeal with them; ſacrifice to them; and, court their ſovereign charms to their laſt breath.

THE END.

ERRATA.

Page 20. Line 13. *for* comma *after* ſays, *place* ſemi-colon.

P. 61. L. 7. *for* Morte *read* Morto.

P. 83. Note, *for* Bernoue *read* Bernoull.

P. 94. L. 3. *after* Nature *add a* colon—*after* flat *add* it.

P. 105. L. 10. *dele* Lucian, Ep. I.

P. 166. Note f. *inſtead of* 'OΔ.T. v. 230. *read* Ψ. v. 163.

P. 181. L. 13. *for* on *read* in.

P. 189. L. 20. *for* or *read* on.

P. 197. Note d. *for* adv. *read* ad v.

P. 227. L. 12. *for* the *read* her.

www.ingramcontent.com/pod-product-compliance
Lightning Source LLC
Chambersburg PA
CBHW020854020726
47497CB00005B/1404